# Vietnam Stories

Tales of Gay experiences during the Vietnam War

# By G.D. Lorentzen

For all gay men and women who serve and have served.

Leo Sun Publications
Portland, OR USA
Printed by www.lulu.com
First edition, 2009

ISBN 978-0-578-03007-4

Cover, Layout & Typesetting by Dan Koperski
www.koperski.com

cover photo by Thomas Skibicki

# contents

# Foreword

I wrote these fictional stories for a couple of reasons. One, I am a Vietnam veteran and I suppose I still had a few demons that needed to be exorcised. Writing the stories using autobiographical elements but with fictional characters helped me pull out some of the left-over slivers in my soul. Here it is four decades later, and I'm still processing my experiences in Vietnam, trying to understand what happened.

Two, I wanted to tell stories about gay soldiers in Vietnam, because we were there and we served and sacrificed like everyone else. I also wanted to show that, based on my personal experiences, being gay was not a deterrent to promotion or good relations with other straight men. The unit leadership was the key to harmonious relations between the gay and straight men, just as it was between Blacks and Whites. Bad leadership always meant conflict between sub-cultural groups within a unit, whether they were racial, sexual, ethnic, religious or whatever. Adherence to the military code of conduct was the common piece that kept the integrity and cohesiveness of the unit. Being gay was not an issue that disturbed that integrity or that cohesion. My friends assumed I was gay, and yet it was never a barrier to our friendship. They teased me, but it was with affection. It was all good natured fun and I was always grateful for their acceptance and inclusion in every social circumstance or event. I was never ostracized and no one ever harassed me, nor did I see any physical violence against any perceived gay man in our unit. But for dramatic purposes and realism, I did include one situation of gay bashing in one of the stories. I left it open to interpretation, though, as to whether it was truly because he was gay or whether there was a personality conflict that led to the violence.

The characters in the stories are based on composite memories of various men I knew in Vietnam. The situations and relationships, although based on my Vietnam experiences and observations, are completely fictional. Any resemblance to any persons living or dead is purely coincidental and unintended.

I would like to dedicate the stories to all veterans of foreign wars, but most specifically to those gay men who served in Vietnam.

G.D. Lorentzen
Portland OR, November 2008

# fixin' to die

G.D. Lorentzen

# Fixin' to Die

Bobby Pinks sat looking out of the airplane window as it began its descent into Bismarck. The North Dakota State Capitol rose unexpectedly from the prairie floor. It looked much taller and grander in this relatively flat environment than its mere eighteen stories would look in a more urban space. As the plane descended, the street pattern came into view amidst the green trees and the trees clearly marked the furthest extent of the small city that spread out on the otherwise treeless plains along the east bank of the Missouri River. He looked down at his seat belt and his Class–A Army uniform momentarily surprised him. Then he remembered. He had actually forgotten for a few moments that he was on his way to Vietnam and he was going home on leave. He leaned his head back against the seat and wondered how he would tell his parents where he was going. He felt the jolt of the wheels hitting the runway and the force of the jet as it strained to slow down. He looked again out of the window and the old terminal, built in the 1930s by New Deal workers, was looking worn and anachronistic in the age of space exploration and Boeing jets. He smiled to himself thinking that his parents were children of the New Deal and were also beginning to appear worn and anachronistic in 1968. He thought more about his parents and he had to admit to himself that they hardly knew each other even after eighteen years together. They couldn't confide in each other and he couldn't really talk to them. He hadn't seen them for nearly ten months and he had no idea how to tell them about Vietnam.

The flight attendant's voice brought him out of his thoughts. "Ladies and Gentlemen, welcome to the Bismarck Municipal Airport. It is 02:25pm Central Daylight Time. Please remain seated until the airplane has come to a complete stop and the fasten seat belt sign has been turned off. We want to thank you for flying Northwest Airlines and wish you a pleasant stay in North Dakota."

The plane came to a stop at the gate, the seat belt sign went off accompanied by an electronic tone, and the passengers began standing and opening the overhead bins to retrieve their luggage. Bobby stayed seated until there was room for him to stand and step into the aisle. He didn't have anything with him in the overhead bin, just his duffle bag, which he had checked when he boarded in Washington, D.C. As he walked down the aisle towards the exit, the flight attendant smiled at him and said, "Bye." Bobby just smiled back and nodded his head, then walked out of the cabin door into the ramp. When he reached the entrance to the terminal, his mother, father and the four oldest of his six siblings were all standing there somewhat off to the side waiting in anticipation. Bobby stepped out of the crowd into view and they smiled and waved with excitement. His mother, Rose, clapped her hands and rushed towards him. She embraced him and gave him a maternal kiss on his left cheek and said with some excitement, "Welcome home, son!"

His dad, Earl, stood behind her, and when she was satisfied with her embrace, she stepped back to allow him access to Bobby. He stuck his hand out to shake Bobby's hand and said, "You look just fine, Bobby. Just fine. So grown up in that uniform!"

"Thanks, Dad," said Bobby a little embarrassed. He knew that his military training had reshaped his body into a young man. He wasn't built like an adolescent anymore. His blond Nordic, five foot eleven frame was slender but not skinny and his dark, blue–gray eyes were more focused than before. He was more observant of and responsive to his environment.

"Come on kids," urged his father. "Come say hello to Bobby. You haven't seen him for more than nine months. Don't be shy now."

The three boys and a girl all walked slowly towards Bobby, then put their arms around his waist looking up at him. Bobby looked down and smiled. He had missed them, but he didn't feel much connection to them anymore. His time in the family suddenly seemed like a long time ago and he realized he had emotionally withdrawn from them since he had been in the Army.

"Hey, kids, come help me get my duffle bag, OK?" he said. "I checked my duffle bag in D.C.," he explained to his parents. And they all walked together to Baggage Claim.

Once he had picked up his duffle bag, they walked to the parking lot and drove home to the south side of town. The family home was a large, old house on Bowen Avenue just off Washington Street near the park. Bobby was born at St. Alexis Hospital on November 2, 1948 at 04:49pm, and he had lived on the south side of Bismarck his entire life. He had gone to Wachter Elementary School and Bismarck High, then joined the Army after high school instead of going on to college. He seemed to be the all–American boy of the 1960s. But whatever was apparent was deception. He never played school sports, preferring just to ice skate in his spare time at the local ice rink or, in the winter, at the neighborhood outdoor ice rink in the park. He never went on a date and he never had a girlfriend, yet no one realized it. He was friendly, sociable and appeared to have a large circle of friends, but this, too, was all shine. He had very few friends. Despite this, others perceived him as the red–blooded all–American boy. He was handsome without being Hollywood, had above average intelligence and was a good student in school. He joined a Military Intelligence unit in the Army. His job was to analyze communications traffic patterns of America's Cold War enemies. This added to his reputation at home and gave him a certain gravitas that other boys his age didn't have. Bobby wasn't completely aware of his own reputation and impact on others around him. He felt shy and awkward on the inside, but projected a confidence that others respected. Now he was on leave before going to Vietnam. He was not sure how friends and neighbors would accept his participation. He knew it was growing more and more unpopular, especially after the Tet Offensive in the previous January.

But it was 1968 and it was his boomer generation's turn to go to war. In spite of the protests against it, there were millions of men who were drafted or volunteered to fight this regional war against the forces of Communism. Bobby Pinks, like most of them, didn't know the history of the conflict. None understood the geopolitical dynamics. None wished any real harm to the Vietnamese. None really wanted to go. And just like Bobby Pinks, millions went. Bobby didn't really know why. After high school he felt he had two choices: college or the military. The American social and political landscape had changed enough that college had become almost necessary to lead a comfortable, middle class life, yet Bobby wasn't emotionally ready for college. He wasn't intellectually prepared for the war, but the risks and the adventure of it resonated enough that he could accept it. It was honorable. It was a young male thing like hockey or football—risky, frisky, aggressive, and disciplined. Bobby loved the young male thing, precisely because he had never participated in it before. There was something about the culture and environment of Bismarck that would not allow him to express himself naturally. In the military, he had no personal history and it was a fresh start for him. And so it was. He made the choice and joined the ranks of the eternal warriors, that archetypal class of men who takes up arms and seeks vengeance in ancient lands while home echoes softly from some place in their memories. Bobby's take on it was romantic, not patriotic.

He spent ten uneventful, boring days with his family. He was somewhat anxious about the war and wanted to get on with it. He had to fly to San Francisco. He didn't tell his parents where he was going until the day before he left. When they asked him why he was home on leave, he simply told them his training was finished and he had ten days to report to his next duty station. Earl and Rose knew something wasn't quite right, but they didn't ask. They never felt that Bobby accepted any probe into his personal affairs. Even as a child, Bobby had a private, if not secret life, into which he never allowed his parents. This time was no different for them. They knew that he was in control of the flow of information. He would tell them what was happening when he decided the time was right. They had always let it be that way. They never pried or pressed him for answers.

Bobby began packing up his things the day before his flight. Rose noticed and helped him with a few things. Bobby stopped for a moment and said to her, "Mom, I'm leaving for San Francisco tomorrow and..."

Rose interrupted him, saying, "That'll be fun, Bobby. Is that where you'll be stationed?"

"Only for a couple weeks, if that," he said. "Then I'm shipping out to Vietnam." Bobby looked at his mother wanting to see a reaction.

Rose paused momentarily while folding his clothes, but quickly picked up the pace. "Earl said it was something like that," she said without looking up. "Well? Are you OK with it?" she asked.

"What do you mean?" Bobby asked obtusely, knowing full well what she meant.

"You're not upset about it?" she asked.

"What's the point? I can't change it," he answered with the resignation clearly expressed in his voice.

"You want me to tell your dad, or do you want to?" she asked looking at him with sympathy.

"No, I can," he said. "It's OK. In fact, let me go do it now."

"He's sitting in the living room," said Rose.

Earl didn't have much of a reaction, when he told him, but Bobby saw the dismay in his eyes. Earl got up from the sofa, his forty–five year old frame just beginning to show the signs of middle age. He slowly walked into the kitchen to the fridge to get a beer. He stayed in the kitchen. Nothing more was said.

The next day they drove him back to the airport. As Bobby was about to board, Rose hugged him and pleaded with him to write. Earl shook his hand and said, as only Earl could say, "Well, Bobby, you're a man now, and you're going off to war. This could be the last time we see each other. You know, you might not come back."

Bobby didn't react to his father's send off. He simply looked at the man slightly disgusted with what he had said. He shook his father's hand, and dismissed his ineptitude and unintentional insensitivity. He smiled a very weak smile, waved briefly at his parents and walked down the ramp onto the plane. He didn't look back, but he knew that his mother was crying.

He flew to San Francisco where he was billeted for seven days at the Presidio just beneath the Golden Gate Bridge. He was there for Vietnam orientation with thirty-six other traffic analysts from Fort Myers, Virginia. They spent six days sitting through lectures and slide shows that familiarized them all with the communication patterns used by the North Vietnamese Army and the Viet Cong.

Bobby stayed mostly to himself at the Presidio. Many guys would take off in the evening to have fun down on Market Street or up in the Tenderloin. Bobby didn't. He wasn't very experienced in big cities and he felt intimidated by San Francisco. He did go out in the early evening to Chinatown to get dinner, because he liked real Chinese food, but then he would go right back to the barracks and spend the rest of the evening reading and watching TV. Besides, Bobby was a good kid—a goody-two-shoes, in fact. Not because he was afraid of getting into trouble, but rather because he was just in his soul a wholesome character. He was civilized and responsible. On his sixth evening at the Presidio, he was sitting in the TV room watching Laugh In, when one of the young men from the orientation walked in and sat down next to him. Bobby didn't know his name, but acknowledged his presence with a nod and a smile. During a commercial, the guy turned to Bobby and said, "Hi. I'm Joey Dee. And you are?"

"Bobby Pinks."

"Oh, right. I think I remember your name from advanced training at Fort Myers," he said, then continued, "my name is actually Joseph Diefenbach, but everyone just calls me Joey Dee."

"Good to meet you," said Bobby. "I remember your name, too. What company were you in?"

"F Troop," answered Joey Dee.

"Oh, OK. I was in Delta Company. I didn't really know anyone in F Company. Did you train as a traffic analyst?"

"Yeah, most everybody did, didn't they?" asked Joey Dee.

"Well, some were doing crypto over at Arlington Station, too," answered Bobby.

"Ah, right. I remember," said Joey Dee. "I didn't pay much attention to all that spook stuff."

Bobby laughed. "What are you doing in Military Intelligence then if you don't pay any attention to it?

"That's actually a funny story," said Joey Dee. "When they said I could be a traffic analyst, I really thought they were talking about transportation, not intelligence gathering and communications traffic."

Bobby smiled and said, "That is funny. Didn't your recruiter explain it?"

"Fuck no," answered Joey Dee with a smile that expressed amusement at his own naivite. "Hell, they hooked me as easy as a catfish. I bought their bullshit hook, line and sinker. I think it's my small-town Ohio gullibility."

Bobby was amused and entertained by Joey's non-judgmental and uncomplicated view of the world. He had forgotten after a year in the military stationed in D.C. how refreshing small-town attitudes were. He was curious why Joey Dee was in the barracks.

"So, how come you're not out on the town tonight with everybody else?" Bobby asked.

"Being from a town like Bowling Green, Ohio, I'm not very comfortable in big cities," he responded with a shrug of his shoulders.

Bobby chuckled and said, "Yeah, I'm from North Dakota, so I'm not experienced with big cities, either. Other than D.C. and that took a while for me to get used to."

"North Dakota?" asked Joey Dee with some skepticism. "I've never met anyone from North Dakota before. There can't be many people there!"

"Not many, no," Bobby responded. The commercial ended and Laugh In came back on. They both watched and laughed at the show and didn't talk again for a while. When the show was over, Bobby turned to Joey Dee and said, "I'm going up to bed. I hear we're probably going to ship out tomorrow from Oakland. I'm going to get some sleep."

"Yeah, I probably will, too," said Joey Dee. "I want to get some sleep before the other guys come stumbling in, making noise and waking me up."

Bobby agreed with a nod of his head and said, "Right. I hope I can sleep through it. See ya tomorrow maybe."

"Yeah, tomorrow," said Joey Dee and they both went their separate ways in the barracks.

Bobby went back to his bunk thinking about Joey Dee. He was a rosy cheeked, blue-eyed young man who had a midwestern simplicity and honesty about him that Bobby liked. He was prettier than he was handsome, yet stocky and masculine without being fat. He had wavy, chestnut-colored hair that cascaded about halfway down his forehead. Bobby noticed it right away, because his hair didn't look regulation. He had also noticed that Joey had a toothy, handsome smile with great dimples. Bobby was intrigued and he looked forward to getting to know him. Bobby got undressed, crawled into bed and promptly fell asleep. If other guys made noise coming in late, Bobby didn't know. He didn't wake up.

The next morning the soldiers were called to formation at 06:00am. Roll was called and they were told to go back to the barracks to retrieve their duffle bags, report to the mess hall, and at 07:30am to be in front of the barracks. Busses would be there to transport them to the Alameda Naval Air Station near Oakland. They would be leaving for Vietnam from there.

Joey Dee found Bobby once they were in the terminal at the Naval Air Station. It was a cavernous hangar without acoustics. The din from the hundreds of talking soldiers was almost unbearable. Bobby was standing with his duffle bag in the middle of the crowd. They had been herded into the hangar to wait for their transports to arrive. Joey Dee noticed him standing alone. He spoke to no one. He just stood there absent-mindedly looking around. Joey Dee made his way through the crowd, walked up to Bobby and said, "Good morning."

Bobby looked a little surprised, then smiled and said, "Morning."

"Ready for this?" asked Joey Dee.

Bobby chuckled and rolled his eyes a little. "I am, actually. I'm tired of the hurry up and wait and just want to get there."

"What?" asked Joey Dee leaning closer to hear better.

"I just want to get there," yelled Bobby with his face very near Joey's.

"I know. Me, too. I'm wondering how long we have to wait here in this hangar," shouted Joey Dee.

"Well, it shouldn't be too long," Bobby shouted back. He leaned over to Joey's ear and yelled, "I heard one of the officers in the barracks say we were leaving at noon. It's 11:15 now, so I bet we board any minute."

Bobby was right. The men were rounded up at 11:30am and assigned to different doors of the hangar. Bobby and Joey Dee lined up together in front of their exit and waited. An officer came forward and led them outside to a waiting plane. As they walked out onto the tarmac they both saw at the same time that they were flying a United Airlines charter with civilian flight attendants. Bobby was dumbfounded that the government would charter a civilian airliner with stewardesses to transport soldiers to a war zone. Bobby and Joey Dee looked at each other with the same quizzical look. They climbed the portable stairs and passed by the United stewardess greeting them with a smile as they walked onto the plane. The irony wasn't lost on the other troops either, and there was a spontaneous expression of their cynicism once the plane began to take off. As they gathered speed down the runway the entire plane load of soldiers broke into a rendition of Country Joe McDonald's "Fixin' to Die Rag."

*One two three, what are we fightin' for?*
*Don't ask me, I don't give a damn!*
*Next stop is Vietnam.*
*Five six seven, open up the pearly gates!*
*Ain't got time to wonder why,*
*Whoopee! We're all gonna die!*

After twenty-two hours and refueling stops in Guam and Tokyo, they finally landed in Saigon. As Bobby stepped off the plane onto the tarmac, the tropical air hit him like a tidal wave of heat and humidity. He had to inhale deeply to feel like he was getting oxygen. He began to sweat immediately and his clothing stuck to his sweaty body. He felt very uncomfortable. Suddenly there was a loud wail of sirens and the sound of heavy thuds accompanied by a small quake under his feet. The realization that the airbase was under mortar attack hit everyone getting off the plane at the same time. Bobby ran like hell across the tarmac and jumped into a trench at the edge of the runway. He looked cautiously over the rim of the trench and saw two tall columns of smoke near the end of the runway. The thuds stopped and the sirens sounded the all clear. As Bobby and a dozen men around him crawled out of the trench, they looked up to see a captain with legs slightly spread, hands on his hips and a grin on his tanned face.

"Welcome to Vietnam!" he said loudly. He looked around at the new men and, laughing, said, "You'll get used to it. Come on. Up off your hands and knees and follow me."

Bobby wondered to himself if this mortar attack was an omen. Did it foreshadow what was to come? Did it mean anything at all? He couldn't shake the feeling that he really was fixin' to die, yet it didn't frighten him. The death he sensed was not a physical death, but rather a profound change in his very young life. As he walked with the group of nugs (new guys), he looked around observing the environment of Ton Son Nhut Airbase: the tarmac, the jets, the planes, the helicopters, the engine noises, jeeps rushing here and there, and the bustling sound of the thousands of soldiers and airmen all contributed to the overwhelming intensity Bobby felt at that moment. He looked straight ahead at the captain leading him into the unknown—into his own personal oblivion—and his mind wanted to turn around and run the other way. Not out of fear exactly, but rather from a feeling that he wasn't prepared. His feet kept him marching forward and he knew he was now a willing participant in a journey through his own personal darkness. He found a panoramic open space in his mind that allowed him to accept the situation without prejudice or any possibility of remorse. It was a watershed moment in his life and he knew it. He was in Vietnam. It was war. He was a significant part of human history. He was there, and he was really OK with it. These realizations brought a sudden end to the old Bismarck Bobby Pinks. As he walked into the Ton Son Nhut terminal, Bobby walked into a new life and a new way of being.

## Kiss me, Joey!

The men went through another typical military processing center in Saigon. Papers, signatures, documents in triplicate, standing in line, waiting, hurrying, and more waiting. After three days, Bobby's group, including Joey Dee, was put on a military transport to Da Nang, their new home for the coming year.

The military intelligence compound at Da Nang looked very well polished and trimmed. This bothered Bobby. In Bobby's experience, any time he saw polish and trim, he knew that the officers had nothing better to do than harass the enlisted men with work detail. This was to be an understatement. The compound at Da Nang wasn't paved. There were simply dirt roads wide enough for trucks and jeeps to negotiate their way through the area. At one end stood the administration building and the mess hall. At the other end stood the operations compound. Along the main road through the company stood the rows of barracks, often called hootches, on each side of the road. There was also a small wooden shack that served as the 'club', where soldiers could get beer, alcohol, soda pop and popcorn. The selection and offerings were very limited, however, and often all that was available to drink were a bitter, watery beer called "Grainbelt", Rooty Tooty Rootbeer and Fanta Orange. Every now and then a shipment of whiskey would come through, but very seldom. Once a week a movie was projected onto a large sheet tacked to one wall. This was the extent of any entertainment in the company, yet it was not the extent of the men's ability to find alternative forms of recreation. This recreation was of prime importance to the men because of the intensity of their work schedules.

Bobby began on-the-job training for his communications analyst position, and after one day, found out that there were men in the company who had worked as long as one hundred and sixty days straight, twelve to fourteen hours a day, without a day off. Bobby had arrived in Da Nang on May 2nd, 1968. He worked until August 4th before he got his first day off. Work details included digging in the sand pits and filling sandbags, raking the powdery, red dirt around the administration and officer's quarters into straight lines, whitewashing large rocks and tree trunks, and guard duty on the perimeter. This was all in addition to the twelve-hour shifts in the operations center analyzing communications traffic.

Not only were the work schedules difficult, the weather unbearable and the officers aggravating, but the enemy dropped rockets and mortars on the compound three or four days a week. This happened usually at night, rousing men out of their cherished sleep and forcing them into the trenches that surrounded the compound. So, in addition to the overall intensity of life in Da Nang, the men were also often sleep deprived.

By the beginning of August 1968, Bobby was intensely depressed and angry. He wanted out. He'd had enough. His patience and good humor no longer existed. He no longer cared about living or dying or war or peace. He only wanted peace of mind and to be left alone. He was burnt out from overwork and the constant trivial harassment from the officers. Da Nang was, in reality, psychological torture and it was beginning to take its toll on Bobby and many others. Joey Dee had begun visiting Bobby more and more often and they became good friends during the first three months of their time in Vietnam. Bobby knew that their friendship was a safe haven from the insanity of their situation. They often talked about it complaining to each other, and the more they talked about their dissatisfaction, the more they became dependent on each other for their sense of well-being. In turn, their sense of well-being became dependent on the state of their relationship.

It was not completely coincidental that they both received their first day off on the same day. They had started their training and work schedule on the same day, so it made sense to them. They were both incredibly excited about the prospects of twenty-four hours without having to go to the compound to work. They decided to meet in the mess hall for breakfast and talk about what they wanted to do for the day. Joey Dee had arrived a few minutes before Bobby and was sitting at a table with his hands around a hot cup of coffee. Bobby came in, looked around, settled his gaze on Joey Dee, smiled and walked in his direction. Joey Dee raised his hand in greeting.

"Morning," he said with some enthusiasm for the day.

"Hey," said Bobby. "You haven't eaten yet?"

"Naw. I thought I'd wait for you. They got french toast for a change," Joey Dee said with a tone of voice that made it sound as if french toast were some exquisite Cordon Bleu specialty.

"Yeah? Good," said Bobby standing at the table. "Let's go get some."

Joey Dee stood up and they went together to the serving area. After loading up with french toast and fresh fruit, they sat back down and ate.

"Any ideas what you want to do today?" asked Bobby with a smile.

"Why don't we go downtown Da Nang, find a restaurant for dinner or something?" he suggested.

"Cool! Da Nang. I hadn't even thought about going down there," said Bobby.

"I'm just thinkin' it'd be fun to do some sightseeing—see something real outside of this fucking company," said Joey Dee.

"I'm with ya there," said Bobby in agreement. "You know, we haven't even been to China Beach yet, either."

"Hey, now there's a thought!" exclaimed Joey Dee. "Let's bring a towel and trunks and maybe we can find our way to the beach."

"I like it. Let's do that," said Bobby grinning with excitement and nodding his head. "I'll go get my things together and I'll meet you in front of the barracks in a few minutes."

"Cool," said Joey Dee. "Don't forget the suntan lotion. I think we're gonna need it."

They got up from the table and walked back to the barracks. As they walked through the center of the company on the main dirt road, the air was pierced by the cracking sound of a weapon being fired. They dropped to the ground in reaction and Joey Dee exclaimed with shock, "What the fuck was that?"

"Sounded like shots fired," answered Bobby facing Joey with his cheek pressed into the dirt. Just then there was a loud commotion near the front door of a nearby hootch and a group of men, obviously fighting with each other, came stumbling out of the door. There were four guys struggling with one soldier who had an M-14 rifle. They struggled with urgency, pressed him to the ground, took the weapon away and held him down. Joey Dee and Bobby stood up after the wild man had been subdued. They dusted themselves off and ran over to them.

"Need any help here?" asked Bobby with concern.

"Call the MPs!" shouted one of the men. "This mother fucker just tried to kill us in the barracks!"

Bobby and Joey Dee ran around the corner to Headquarters and reported the incident. Once the MPs were called, they ran back to the scene. The MPs came immediately after they had returned. The soldier on the ground was still being held down and had stopped struggling against the strength of the four other men on top of him.

"What's wrong with that guy?" asked Joey Dee amazed at the scene unfolding before his eyes.

"We don't know, for sure," said one of the guys slightly out of breath. "He apparently got a Dear John letter from his fiancée and went crazy. Tried to kill everybody around him and himself."

"Fuckin' psycho, man!" Bobby said shaking his head. Three MPs arrived on the scene with weapons drawn.

"Come on, son," said one of the MPs, who was clearly older and a lifer in the Army. He pushed the other guys off of him, and with the help of the other two MPs, handcuffed him and led the young soldier away.

Joey Dee and Bobby looked at each other, shook their heads and walked towards their own barracks. They didn't speak for a few minutes until they had reached the barracks door.

"That's fucked up," said Joey Dee. "Snapping like that over a Dear John letter."

"That's for sure," responded Bobby with a heavy sigh. "Come on. Let's get the fuck outta here. I need to get away from here for a while."

"Me, too," said Joey Dee. "Let's get our stuff and go to the beach. I'm really looking forward to hearing the ocean again."

They got their towels and trunks, met each other at the door and walked out of the compound gate. It was the first time they had left the company area since arriving in Da Nang. They both felt a little lighter, a little less burdened and less stressed once they were on the outside.

There were no normal taxis in Da Nang as an American might think of them. The Vietnamese drove three-wheeled Italian Lambrettas. Once outside of the compound and on the streets of Da Nang, it was easy to hail a Lambretta from just about any corner. Bobby and Joey Dee just stood for a moment on the street corner looking like they were going somewhere, and a pale blue Lambretta pulled up and the driver asked, "Where you go, G.I.?"

"China Beach," answered Bobby somewhat tentatively.

"Get in. I take you," said the driver. "Three MPC." MPC were military payment certificates used in the local economy instead of greenbacks. This made black marketeering a little more difficult, but only a little.

Bobby looked at Joey Dee and shrugged his shoulders. Joey Dee nodded his head in agreement and they both got in the back of the vehicle, which was covered but open on the sides. It took about twenty minutes to drive through the bustling streets of Da Nang, choking on the exhaust of the thousands of Lambrettas fighting for dominance with the bicycles on the roads. Bobby handed the driver three MPC when he dropped them off on the access road to the beach. Bobby and Joey Dee ran down the road, whooping and laughing at the excitement of seeing the ocean and jumping in the surf. When they got to the beach itself, they saw the expansive stretch of white sand dotted with many beach towels and sunbathers. There were a lot of people, including European, Australian and American women in swimwear, walking up and down the beach. Vietnamese women were also there carrying baskets filled with freshly cut pineapples that they sold for fifty cents a piece. Joey Dee and Bobby located a sparsely populated spot, laid down their towels and ran into the surf. They played, swam, jumped the waves and dove under the crystal blue waters of the South China Sea. The farther out they swam, the more colorful, tropical fish they could see under the water. They couldn't open their eyes for too long, though, because the salt water irritated them quickly. After an hour or so of swimming, they walked back to their towels and lay next to each other in the sun.

"It's a little surreal here, isn't it?" Joey Dee asked.

"Yeah, I guess so," Bobby said in response. "It's just weird seeing all these civilians on the beach like they were on vacation, y'know?"

"That's what I meant," Joey Dee said still questioning. "Why are they here, I wonder?"

Bobby scanned the beach looking for an answer. "I don't get it, either. Girls in bikinis on the beach in the middle of a war zone like it's not even happening."

"Well, I'm glad we're on the beach and not in the jungles," Joey Dee said looking at Bobby with a grin. "This is kinda nice!"

"It is. It's hot, too," Bobby remarked looking up at the blue sky and bright tropical sun above them.

After lying in the tropical heat for only a few minutes, the ocean water had evaporated and their skin was dry. Joey Dee reached into his little bag to pull out the suntan lotion. "Bobby, would you put this on my back? I want to lie on my stomach a while."

"Sure. Roll over," said Bobby taking the bottle of suntan lotion and squeezing a dollop in his hand. He spread the white cream across Joey Dee's back and rubbed it in with circular motions. Once he had coated Joey's entire back, he lay on his right side with his elbow in the sand and rested his head in his hand. Joey Dee turned his head to face Bobby and they were much closer to each other than expected. With a sudden impulse, Bobby leaned forward slightly, kissed Joey Dee lightly on the lips and leaned back again.

Joey Dee looked at him very perplexed and said, "That was weird. What was that for?"

When Bobby realized what he had done, he turned bright red, collapsed on his back and said, " I don't know. It just came over me and I...I..."

"You kissed me, man! What the fuck?" exclaimed Joey Dee sitting up.

"I know," answered Bobby somewhat distantly. "I don't know why I did it. This feeling just came over me and I had to kiss you."

"You queer?" asked Joey Dee in a voice filled with disdain.

"Queer? I...I don't know...I never thought about it. Not like that anyway," said Bobby.

"Not like what?" asked Joey Dee.

"Well, not like...I don't know...not like queer...but with you...it just seemed like a natural thing to do," said Bobby turning his head to look at Joey Dee. He felt an implicit trust in Joey Dee that he could just tell him anything.

"What does that mean, Bobby?" asked Joey Dee with concern. "You tellin' me you're in love with me?" Joey leaned towards Bobby with expectation.

"I don't know, Joey," said Bobby sitting up next to him looking perplexed. "But I kissed you, didn't I, and, honestly, it just felt like the right thing to do."

"Bobby, no...no...you just can't do that!" said Joey Dee with deep concern. "You can't go around kissing your friends just because you want to. You'll get your ass kicked. And if you do it to me again, I'll kick your ass myself!"

Bobby looked carefully at Joey Dee and saw a genuine disturbance on his face. Bobby could not accept that Joey was truly upset. Although never articulated, Bobby assumed they had an unconditional friendship. The fact that Joey Dee could be upset over this, disturbed Bobby.

"Sorry. It won't happen again," said Bobby obviously upset. He grabbed his things and stood up. "Maybe we should go."

"Bobby, lay your ass back down here and let's just forget it," said Joey Dee attempting to smooth the situation.

"No, I can't, " said Bobby. "I kissed you for a reason and, ah, it's just the way I felt at that moment. It was just something for you and me, nobody else. But you don't feel that way, right?"

"Feel what way?" asked Joey Dee. "You mean, like kissing you back?"

"Yeah. Kissing me back," said Bobby looking down at him expecting to hear what he wanted to hear.

"You're fuckin' crazy," said Joey Dee rolling over on his stomach and facing away from him.

"So, you aren't interested in kissing me," said Bobby with more of an edge in his voice.

"Get off it, Bobby," said Joey Dee angrily.

Something came over Bobby at that moment. He was incensed. He could not understand why Joey Dee would be so angry over this. He felt confrontational—aggravated.

"Tell me to my face that you don't want to kiss me," challenged Bobby.

Joey Dee rolled over, stood up and faced Bobby almost nose to nose. He pushed Bobby's upper chest with his right index finger and said, "I don't want to kiss you, Bobby. I'm not going to kiss you and you aren't going to kiss me again, either. Is that clear?"

Bobby was embarrassed and looked down, but he didn't say anything. Joey Dee took a deep breath, exhaled, and said, "Now sit your ass down on that towel and let's get some sun, OK? You're my friend, all right? And that's all we're ever going to be, got it?"

Bobby nodded and sat down on the towel. He felt very disappointed and rejected. Although he had never consciously thought about his feelings for Joey Dee, he felt a deep love for him and, in his self-absorbed way, thought Joey Dee had to love him, too, in the same way. It's what made sense to him. For Joey Dee to reject Bobby's advances put their relationship at risk. Now he was afraid he might have ruined their friendship, and having him as a friend was far better than not having him around at all. He looked over at Joey lying there on his back facing the sun with his eyes closed.

"I'm sorry, Joey," he apologized quietly. "I really am. I won't do it again, I promise."

Joey Dee didn't open his eyes or look at Bobby. He simply lay there and said with a milder tone, "You're damned right you won't. Now shut up about it, OK?"

Bobby's behavior towards Joey Dee had crossed the line, true, but Joey Dee did not perceive it as much of a threat, because he really was not thinking about Bobby as gay. He did not think about homosexuals in terms of civil or human rights. He really didn't think about them at all. He just didn't take them all that seriously. In Joey Dee's hometown in Ohio, there were such questionable characters around, but they were part of the fabric of the community. They were accepted as human beings albeit marked with scarlet and lavender letters. There was the pervert who always exposed himself to children. Joey and his childhood friends had often giggled about him with hands over their mouths and eye contact that expressed the childish titillation of illicit knowledge. There was an old timer who had spent many years in prison for manslaughter. Local kids were afraid of him because of the rumors and avoided him like Scout avoided Boo Radley in *To Kill a Mockingbird*. There was a middle-aged woman who had given birth out of wedlock when she was younger. The upstanding women of the town clucked their tongues and walked the other way, if they ran into her in the grocery store. Yet, when she had an emergency appendectomy, many of these same disapproving women were the first to visit her and bring her flowers. There were a few alcoholics who often had to be driven home after the bars closed. There were the local queers who would cruise each other in the rest area just off the highway outside of town and whose names would be in the newspaper if caught by the police. Everyone knew who they were. Joey knew who they were. One was the head librarian. Another was the town auditor. People knew and disapproved of these men, but they were still part of the social fabric of the town. There was even a priest who often had to ask to be taken from a local bar back to the priory on Saturday night before midnight. These people all had some mark against them and now and then some of them were arrested and put in the town jail, yet they were never fully ostracized from the community at large.

Joey Dee was always warned who was 'strange' and whom he should stay away from. Parents monitored this carefully. The community simply kept its eyes on these questionable characters, but the important thing was, the community always took care of its own. In many respects, this was the Christian nature of their small town culture. It went somewhat beyond tolerance. For the most part, the townspeople recognized the sin, but acceptance of it as the fundamental truth of human nature was more important than rejecting the sinner. They had to live together in the town after all. So, for Joey Dee to realize there was something queer about Bobby, it just didn't occur to him that he should reject Bobby for it. It was not the way of his small-town midwestern upbringing. These socially questionable people added color and texture to life in the community, even if such people suffered because of their status and had to remain somewhat invisible, while others whispered about them and watched them carefully.

So it was that Joey Dee could lie there on the beach next to Bobby for another hour or so, without being terribly concerned or upset. When they'd had enough sun, they decided to find a restaurant to get some dinner. Bobby kept his eye on Joey Dee to see if his attitude towards him had changed. Joey Dee behaved as if nothing had happened. They simply carried on that afternoon as the friends they had become. For Bobby, however, he was slowly coming to the realization that he had feelings for Joey that he should examine. At that moment, he didn't, and after a few hours and then days, he nearly forgot about those feelings. He was also relieved after a few days, when Joey Dee still came around and they still hung out together in their free time.

## Pinks' Triangle

The young men in the unit found all kinds of ways to divert their attention away from the war. Drinking, smoking marijuana, doing drugs, and having sex with prostitutes were the usual diversions. These were all the ways guys tried to make themselves feel better. Bobby and Joey Dee didn't really involve themselves too much in all of that. They stayed relatively aloof from the more bizarre behavior of their friends and colleagues. The veneer of civilization on these young men was wearing very thin. Bobby and Joey Dee remembered the guy who was so burnt out, his overreaction to a Dear John letter so extreme, that he opened fire in his barracks trying to kill his bunkmates. Later, another became so despondent he killed himself with an M-16 rifle set on automatic. Others would go on sick-call every other day. Still others would get crazy drunk at night and go on rampages, and there were those completely lost souls who held 'gross out contests' as a diversion from the misery of their daily lives. The worst Bobby and Joey Dee ever witnessed was during monsoon season when the seepage from the latrines and piss tubes would cover the ground with a green slime. There were bets placed on men racing from the latrine to the piss tube in an alligator crawl through the muck.

In this stressful, degenerate environment, Bobby withdrew from the company of most of his colleagues and found some level of comfort and solace only in his developing friendship with Joey Dee. Joey Dee was just as uncomfortable with the general behavior of the men in the company and needed Bobby's friendship as much as Bobby needed his. They would often pull their work details together and any free time they had, they would spend together at the club, that make-shift wooden shack with a bar, a popcorn machine, a refrigerator and a few tables and chairs. They occupied their time outside of work and details watching movies, eating popcorn and drinking Rooty Tooty Rootbeer. They both preferred to develop close friendships, be together with those friends and, in reality, take refuge in those relationships. Bobby, especially, became very attached to his friends in Vietnam. Maybe too attached. He found himself becoming emotionally involved with Joey Dee. He couldn't seem to separate love and friendship in his emotional life. Through his relationship with Joey Dee, he gained some insight into what his issues were. He was making acquaintances in the unit, but Joey Dee had become the closest friend and their relationship was the most healing and helpful. Bobby knew he loved Joey, but he didn't really understand what that meant. And although the disturbance in their friendship caused by the kiss on the beach had passed, Bobby still had not come to terms with his attachment to Joey. He didn't completely understand Joey's other relationships and friendships or that their friendship was still vulnerable, precisely because he was falling in love with him. That realization would soon come to him as result of their time spent at the club.

Bobby found the opportunity to learn Vietnamese from the club waitress there. He had bought some books from the University of Saigon, and Lien, the popcorn girl, recently hired by the Supply Officer, agreed to teach him the language. She was nineteen and very beautiful. Bobby and Joey Dee always went there together and they became good friends with Lien. Lien and Bobby seemed to be closer because he was making such an effort to learn her language. Joey Dee would often just sit there, listen, and not say anything unless there was an opportunity to speak English. Bobby didn't realize it at the time, but Joey Dee was falling in love with Lien. They would glance at each other behind Bobby's back or over his head. They would smile and nod at each other as if there were some secret they possessed. It was par for the course, because Bobby was falling more deeply in love with Joey Dee. Over time, he could tell that Lien had feelings for Joey Dee, too, and Bobby began feeling a little jealous. He never examined the source of his jealousy though. He knew it, but wouldn't admit to himself that he was, in fact, in love with Joey Dee. Joey Dee was becoming more deeply involved everyday and he and Lien were spending more and more time alone together. This was a serious problem. If anyone had found out that Joey Dee was having this affair with Lien, he would have lost his security clearance, been removed from Military

Intelligence and sent to a regular Army unit, probably in the infantry.

One day right after work, Bobby walked over to Joey Dee's bunk at a time when he should have been there. He was gone. Somewhat puzzled, Bobby went looking for him. As he walked through the compound towards the club, he saw Bobby and Lien walk out from behind the club and go in the front door. Bobby knew instantly it didn't look right. He picked up his pace, reached the club and walked in. His heart was pounding a little and he felt anxious. Consciously, he knew he was feeling jealousy, but he still denied it to himself for the most part, and still wanted to stop their relationship. He knew he could pull the security clearance card and pressure Joey Dee to step back.

"Hey, guys!" greeted Bobby without revealing any of his feelings.

"Hi, Bobby," said Joey Dee from his perch on a stool at the bar. "It's a bit early to be in the club, isn't it?" Lien turned around and got busy with the popcorn machine pretending not to be interested in their conversation.

"Yeah, guess so," answered Bobby. "But you're here, too. Why so early?"

"Lien and I wanted to talk," said Joey Dee looking across the bar at her. Lien looked up and smiled. "Bobby, we need to tell you something."

"OK, what?" asked Bobby trying to look innocent and oblivious.

"Lien and I are in love," said Joey Dee looking at Bobby for a reaction.

Bobby smiled and looked down, then looked up at Joey. "Nice. You know what you're doing, Joey?" he asked in a serious tone.

"Naw, probably not. But I'm doing it anyway," he said sincerely.

"Yeah..." Bobby broke off his thought. He didn't want to get into the discussion in front of Lien. "Well, as long as you know what you're doin'," he said trying to sound upbeat, but he was hurting. He had known already, but to have Joey Dee confirm it was hard on him.

He looked at Lien making popcorn and realized he desperately needed to get away from them. His feelings were intensifying and he was scared he would reveal himself. "Well, uh, I'll see you two later then, OK? And, uh, congratulations, I guess." Bobby said. Then quickly changing the subject, Bobby simply announced, "I'm gonna get some dinner and write some letters. See ya tomorrow, Lien."

"What about your Vietnamese lesson this evening?" Lien asked a little surprised.

Bobby had forgotten the agreement to have a lesson. He looked at Joey then back at Lien and said, "It's OK. I'm not ready for the next one anyway. Let me work some more on the stuff we've been doing and, ah, when I feel ready, you can teach me some more."

"OK," Lien said a little suspicious of Bobby's reasons.

"Later, Bobby," Joey Dee said.

"Bye, Bobby," added Lien glancing at Joey Dee.

And Bobby walked out of the club. He wondered to himself, if Joey would voluntarily leave Military Intelligence and willingly be reassigned, if it meant he and Lien could be together. He walked slowly toward the mess hall deep in thought when he heard the ominous whistling of an incoming shell.

The sound quickly ripped him away from his thoughts. His instincts grabbed him and he found himself face first in the red, talcum powder–like dirt. Just then a tremendous thud and explosion occurred behind him. He covered his head with his arms and waited. More whistles. More thuds. More explosions. Maybe five or six. He couldn't focus enough to count. Then silence. He waited a minute or two, then stood up, dusted himself off and turned around. He could clearly see that the front of the club was severely damaged. He panicked! He kept repeating to himself as he started running back to the club, "No, my God, no! Fuck no!" When he got to the club, the door was nearly ripped off, windows were shattered and there were shrapnel marks all over the front of it. There was a large crater nearby clearly marking the impact of the mortar. He knew it was a mortar, because it wasn't as big as a rocket crater, nor was the damage as serious. He walked into the club, now filled with the smell of smoke and dust. Joey was lying on the floor and Bobby could see blood. He ran over to him, knelt down and touched him. Joey moaned and opened his eyes. He was alive. Bobby checked his arms and legs, torso and head for possible shrapnel wounds, but only found one cut along the back of Joey's head. It was bleeding profusely, but there was no shrapnel and Bobby realized the wound was relatively superficial. Just his scalp was creased possibly by a sharp piece of shrapnel or maybe hitting the bar as he fell. Bobby sat back on his haunches and sighed with relief.

"Hey, Joey Dee. It's me, Bobby," he said gently pushing on his chest.

Joey Dee looked up and smiled. "Hi. I'm OK, right? I don't know what happened, man. Just sitting here one minute and now I'm looking at you from the floor. It stinks like smoke and fire in here, too."

"Yeah. A mortar," said Bobby quietly. "But I think you're OK. It looks like you hit your head or something, because you're bleeding, but there's no shrapnel anywhere in or on your body, so I think you'll be fine. You're a lucky son-of-a-bitch!"

"Yeah, OK, if this is lucky, you got a strange sense of luck, my friend," said Joey still looking up at Bobby's face.

Bobby smiled down at him and said, "I know. Stupid thing to say, huh? It's what you're supposed to say though in this situation, right?"

"Yeah, it's what you're supposed to say," responded Joey Dee turning his head towards the bar. "How's Lien?"

"I haven't seen her," Bobby answered anxiously. "Let me look behind the bar."

Bobby stood up and looked over the bar. Lien was lying on her stomach on the floor and not moving. He quickly jumped onto the bar and down the other side. About that time, the company Executive Officer and a couple of men came in the club to check out the damage. The Ex-O was a younger, early 30's, average-looking man of average stature. He had been in ROTC in college and received a degree in Math. Now he was a Captain in the U.S. Army and the executive officer of a military intelligence unit. Although he had not been trained in the infantry, he was becoming used to dealing with the high stress, high anxiety rocket and mortar attacks in Da Nang. His steel gray eyes surveyed the room. When he saw Joey Dee on the floor he turned to the two other soldiers with him.

"Get on the phone and get some medics here, asap!" he ordered with urgency. One of the enlisted men with the Ex-O, turned and ran back to Headquarters. The officer knelt down next to Joey Dee and asked, "You OK, soldier?"

Joey Dee nodded yes and said, "I'm just bleeding a bit, but I don't think it's serious."

Bobby stood up and told the officer, "Lien is back here and she's hurt, too."

"Is it bad, Bobby?" asked Joey Dee with concern.

"I don't know, Joey. The medics will have to figure that, I think," Bobby answered.

Four medics ran in the door with gurneys and first aid bags. They went to work immediately on Joey and Lien.

"The girl's OK," said the medic behind the bar. "It knocked her out and she has a couple of superficial scrapes on her shoulders, maybe from small, flying pieces of shrapnel, but it doesn't look like she's been badly hit. The concussion probably knocked her out."

Lien woke up as two medics moved her onto the gurney to take her to the field hospital. The other two did the same for Joey Dee. Bobby followed the medics to the van outside and stood there while they were loaded into the back. Lien was crying. Joey Dee tried to comfort her by saying, "Lien, I think it's OK. We're going to be OK."

"He's right, Lien," Bobby said in agreement. "You're gonna be OK."

Bobby walked up to the driver of the medical van and asked, "Can I catch a ride to the hospital with you guys? These are my friends. I want to be with them until I know they're really OK."

"Sure, hop in," said the driver. And they drove off to the Army field hospital near China Beach.

At the hospital, Bobby waited until a doctor came to explain their conditions. Both were OK. There were no serious wounds and Bobby sighed with relief. He went in to see Lien first. He walked up to her hospital bed in the women's ward, took her hand and greeted her in Vietnamese, "Chao, Lien, co manh gioi? Hi, Lien, how are you feeling?"

"Bay gio, manh gioi. I'm fine now," she said. "Now that I know I'm not seriously hurt. Is Joey Dee doing OK?"

"He'll be fine," Bobby answered. "I think the concussion just knocked him against the bar and he lost consciousness for a few minutes, but otherwise he wasn't hit by shrapnel or anything."

"That's good," she said.

Switching to English, Bobby said, "Lien, I realize this is probably really bad timing, but do you know what could happen to Joey Dee, if anyone found out about you two?"

"What do you mean?" she asked. "Vietnamese girls marry American soldiers all the time."

"I know, but because of Joey Dee's job—he does special work in the Army—secret work—he's not allowed to marry a Vietnamese girl," Bobby explained.

"Not allowed? What will happen?" she asked surprised.

"Well, he will be sent away from here and away from you, probably to an infantry unit," answered Bobby.

"They send him away?" asked Lien with shock in her voice.

"Yes, he will lose his job and the Army will make sure he doesn't see you again," Bobby said. Lien began to cry.

"I'm sorry, Lien," said Bobby with genuine sincerity. "I just thought you should know."

Lien nodded her head and closed her eyes. Bobby patted her hand and said, "I'm going to go see him now, OK? I'll come back later."

"OK," she said. "Come back, though, Ok?"

"I will. I promise," said Bobby and he walked away down the center of the ward. He had told Lien the truth, but he couldn't help feeling guilty. He knew what he had told her was a manipulation, true or not. Bobby was trying to interfere in their relationship, partly out of a sincere fear that Joey Dee would be forced out of Military Intelligence and sent away, and partly out of his own jealousy, although he was still somewhat in denial of his real feelings for Joey Dee. He walked through the swinging doors into the hallway, turned left and headed for the men's ward.

When Joey Dee saw him walking down the center aisle, he sat up with a smile and asked, "Is Lien doing OK?"

Bobby smiled and nodded his head yes. "How are you?" he asked.

"I'm OK," said Joey Dee shrugging his shoulders. "Just a little woozy from being knocked out, I guess. The back of my head hurts under this bandage, but otherwise I'm OK."

"Lien wants you to come and see her as soon as you can," Bobby reported.

"Sure. As soon as I feel like standing up," said Joey Dee.

"I'll come back later if you want me to, and help you walk over to her ward," offered Bobby.

"Thanks, but I think I'll be OK to walk over there," answered Joey.

"OK. Pretty crazy, huh, getting hit by a mortar," said Bobby.

"I'm just happy we weren't really hit. The doctor said the concussion knocked us out for a minute that's all. They checked us for internal injuries, but we're both OK, I guess," explained Joey.

"Yeah, the doctor told me you'd be OK," agreed Bobby. "All the shrapnel hit the front of the club and just a couple pieces hit inside. So, it missed you two."

Joey Dee laid himself back down and gently placed his head on the pillow to avoid too much pressure on the back of his head. "I guess we were pretty lucky after all. Just a couple more feet and it would've been a direct hit on the club and who knows if I'd even be here now."

Bobby reached over and touched his arm. "Yeah, I'm really glad you're going to be OK, Joey."

Joey turned his head to look at him. He put his hand on Bobby's and said, "I know, Bobby. I'm glad you were there when I came to." He smiled then and Bobby smiled back.

"So, when do you think you'll be released from here?" asked Bobby.

"Actually, I'm feeling pretty good, so I think I'll be able to leave as soon as the doctor checks me again," answered Joey. "He's supposed to come back early tomorrow morning, so I should be back in my hooch tomorrow sometime."

"I promised Lien I'd come back this evening to see her before I went back to the barracks, so I'm gonna go over there again for a few minutes. I'll see you in the morning then," said Bobby.

"See ya in the morning," said Joey.

Bobby left and went back to the women's ward. Lien was lying there staring at the ceiling.

She heard the footsteps coming down the center aisle and she turned to see who was coming. She smiled when she saw Bobby.

"Hey," greeted Bobby. Lien just smiled. Bobby continued, "Joey Dee says he'll be released tomorrow morning after the doctor checks him out. So, you'll probably be released, too."

"I think so," said Lien. "Is Joey going to come here to see me?" she asked.

"He said he would as soon as he can stand up without feeling dizzy," Bobby answered with genuine concern in his voice.

"Is he OK?" asked Lien with sudden concern.

"He's OK, Lien," answered Bobby. "He'll be over to see you tonight before you sleep."

Lien looked relieved and said, "That's good. I have to talk to him."

"Well, I need to go now, if that's OK," said Bobby. "I need to get some sleep. I have to be at work at eight tomorrow morning. I hope you get a good night's sleep."

"Cam on," thank you, she said in Vietnamese.

"See you tomorrow?" asked Bobby.

"Khong biet," I don't know, she answered. "I have to think about things."

"I know," said Bobby. "I'm sorry all of this is happening."

"It's not your fault," she said.

"Well, I still feel bad about everything," said Bobby.

"You need to sleep. It's late," she said. "I'm tired, too."

"OK, good night, Lien."

"Good night."

And Bobby left the ward and returned to the barracks. He wondered what Lien would tell Joey Dee. He guessed that she would end the relationship, but he didn't know for sure.

Joey Dee got up out of bed and felt well enough to walk to Lien's ward. When he got to her hospital bed, she sat up and took his hand.

"I'm really glad you're OK," she said. "But that bandage on your head makes it look like you've been wounded."

"I know, but I'm fine," Joey said. "I wanted to come over and see how you were doing."

"Bobby told me," she said. "Come. Sit down next to me."

Joey Dee sat down on the bed. Lien leaned forward looking directly into Joey's eyes and said, "Tell me what happens to you, if you tell your captain that you love me."

Joey realized that she knew something. His expression changed to concern and he answered, "I can't lie to you, Lien. I'll probably have to go to another company somewhere."

Lien nodded and asked, "Will they try to keep us apart?"

Joey looked at her and said, "I suppose at first we can't be together. But after a while, I think it will be OK."

"You think?" she asked. "They send you away and I never see you again."

"Maybe not, Lien," said Joey with hope in his eyes and his voice.

"You hope and you dream," said Lien. "But you don' know."

Joey Dee dropped his head and said, "No, I don't know for sure."

"Joey, this is no good for you," said Lien. "You're in the Army and you can't be with me. I know this."

"Lien, we can work it out somehow," said Joey. "I know we can."

"No, Joey, we can't," she responded. Lien's eyes welled with tears but she didn't cry. "We can be friends and I am honored to be your friend. But we can't be together. It's bad for you. You didn't tell me this. But I know."

Joey was devastated, but he knew it had to be this way. He stood up and said, "Bobby told you?"

Lien nodded and watched Joey as he began walking away from her bed.

"It's true," he said. "They would send me away, but you have to know that Bobby told you this for his own reasons. I would let them send me away and try to have you come to me later. I still think that will work," Joey pleaded with tears in his eyes.

Lien shook her head and said, "No, Joey. I can't wait. My country has a war. I don't know what will happen tomorrow. So, I can't promise that I can come to you in a year or two years or how do we know how many years? You are here for only one year then you go home anyway. When you go home, you won't feel the same, and it will take long time for me to come to you. Too long."

Joey knew that Lien was right and trying to protect him. There were no guarantees in this situation. It was war. He would be home in nine months and it would probably take much longer than that to arrange any reunion with her. It still hurt him to have to let go. He just nodded his head and asked, "When will I see you again?"

"I don't know, Joey," she answered. "I think I don't want to work more in the club. I have my worker I.D. card, so I can find another job for the Americans somewhere else."

Joey suspected then that their relationship was over and he would probably never see her again. He felt empty and drained. The last few hours had taken their toll on him. He just wanted to sleep. "OK, but I'm going to miss you, Lien," he said quietly. He turned around and without looking back walked out of the ward back to his own hospital bed where he fell asleep as soon as his head was on the pillow. Somewhere in his mind, he really didn't believe it was the end of their relationship. His optimism arose as it always did and he couldn't think about the possibility of losing her.

Lien leaned back in her bed and wiped the tears off her cheeks. She really did believe—no, she really did know—it was the end of their relationhip. It hurt, but she knew she would have to bring all of this to a close. Joey Dee would not, of that she was sure. She rang for the nurse and asked for paper, pen and an envelope.

The doctor came in early and woke Joey up. He examined Joey and gave him a clean bill of health. He had, in fact, hit his head on the bar as he fell backwards. He would be fine. Joey got back to the barracks about seven and went to Bobby's bunk. He was still asleep. Joey reached down and gently woke him up. Bobby rolled over to see Joey standing over him.

"Joey," he said. "Wow, you're back!"

"Yeah, come on, man, you gotta get up! Don't you have to be at ops at eight? He asked as he pulled Bobby's covers back.

"Yeah, OK, I'm up," Bobby said as he stood up and stretched.

"I'm going to go to my cubicle and lie down for a while yet. Come see me when you're back from work, OK?" said Joey Dee.

"OK," said Bobby as he watched Joey leave. He called after him, "I'll come by right after chow then." Joey just nodded his head and didn't look back. He was still thinking about his conversation with Lien, Bobby's interference, and grieving over the demise of the relationship.

Right after work, Bobby decided not to go eat. Instead he went to Joey's bunk and found him there sitting cross-legged on his bed crying. It looked like he had been crying all day. He looked up at Bobby, wiped his eyes and holding up a letter said, "Lien called it off...something you said to her...the clearance, work, Military Intelligence and everything."

Bobby didn't respond. He just stood there in silence watching him. He felt an overwhelming affection for him at that moment and he felt really sorry. He knew the letter contained Lien's good-bye.

"Is there anything I can do?" Bobby asked quietly.

Joey looked at him very closely, but without anger, said, "You've done enough. You weren't very supportive and you obviously weren't happy for us, and that helped convince Lien to call it off." He paused, looked away with tears in his eyes and now showing a little anger, said, "You did it out of jealousy, didn't you?"

"Jealousy? I'm really sorry, Joey," Bobby said sincerely surprised. "But I was worried that you'd do something stupid, because you were in love. What do you mean, jealousy? I'm not interested in Lien, and I don't think I've ever done anything to make you think that," he defended himself. His level of anxiety was indicated by the degree of redness rising up his throat and his face. He knew what jealousy Joey Dee meant, but he could not consciously acknowledge it. He felt the need to defend himself.

Joey Dee, still looking away from Bobby, said very quietly, almost as if he didn't want him to hear, "I didn't mean Lien. I was talking about your feelings for me."

Bobby heard it clearly enough and became very embarrassed. His heart raced and his face completely flushed. He couldn't say anything. So many thoughts and emotions churned through his head that he couldn't find one simple or logical enough explanation to give. He sat down on the floor, rested his elbows on his folded legs, placed his chin on his two fists and stared at the floor.

Joey Dee looked at him and realized he was upset. "I'm sorry, Bobby," he said, "I didn't mean to embarrass you, but you know what I'm talking about. You and I have been close enough friends for me to see what's really going on with you, and you can't hide those feelings from me. I'm a little upset, though, that you used those feelings to keep Lien and me apart. I really wish you hadn't done that."

Bobby didn't know what to say. After a few minutes of silence, he stood up to leave. Before he reached the door, Joey Dee said," You know, it's not a problem for me. I'm not going to create a problem for you. I don't want to lose your friendship, but you have to know I don't feel that way about you."

Bobby just nodded his head and said, "I know. I'm sorry. I just never meant to hurt you or Lien." He turned and walked to the door.

"I know," said Joey Dee. "But you did. And I don't think Lien will change her mind now."

"No," Bobby agreed. He did not want to talk about any of this. He needed to get away. "Probably not. Look, uh, I should go. I'll see y'around, huh?"

"Yeah. See ya around," Joey Dee responded slightly annoyed.

And Bobby walked out of his room. He felt very confused and unworthy. He realized he had done something that was unforgivable, at least in his opinion it was. He also concluded that Joey Dee had pointed out something that he was only vaguely aware of. Joey Dee was able to see something in Bobby that wasn't in clear focus from his own subjective point of view. He was now forced to face the fact that he was in love with Joey Dee. He consciously said it to himself. He admitted to himself that Joey Dee was right about him. He thought back to the kiss on the beach and how he had suppressed those feelings and thoughts after Joey Dee rejected his attentions. He learned the real value of friendship and relationship at that moment.

He realized that his friendship with Joey Dee provided a mirror into parts of himself that he couldn't see. Joey Dee gave him feedback about himself that he could not know from the inside. Joey Dee taught him a lot about himself at that moment and he was grateful. Bobby walked to the mess hall and by the time he got there was feeling better. He still knew he had handled the situation badly, but he also knew that Joey still liked him, and hadn't rejected him as a friend. He ate dinner in silence, went back to his bunk and stayed to himself the rest of the evening. He kept thinking about himself as a 'queer.' He was in love with another guy, and consciously admitting that fact, forced him to put it in the context of 'queer.' Objectively, he struggled with the idea and the label. Subjectively, he felt completely normal being in love with Joey Dee. It felt wonderful but at the same time, under the circumstances, bittersweet. He fell asleep that night trusting that Joey Dee was telling him the truth that he didn't care Bobby was queer. He also wondered how many other guys in the unit were queer and whether he was alone.

In the morning, Bobby got up, showered, went to breakfast and then to work, but for the first time in months he didn't stop by Joey Dee's bunk to wake him up. Bobby was self-conscious and contrite enough to feel that he needed to keep his distance and not insert himself into Joey Dee's life anymore. Joey woke up half expecting to see Bobby, but Bobby never came. Joey had to stay away from work for a few more days to recover, according to his doctor's orders. He got up, took his bandage off of his head and showered. Afterwards he rewrapped his head wound and went back to his bunk. He was missing Bobby, but he also didn't want Bobby misunderstanding his feelings for him. He spent the day thinking about the situation and what had happened. He decided to talk to Bobby more about it if he came by after work. Bobby didn't come by, though, which made Joey Dee uncomfortable. He wanted Bobby to come by and visit him. He wanted their normal conversations and mutual companionship. About eight in the evening, after Bobby hadn't showed up, Joey Dee put his boots on and walked over to Bobby's cubicle. He pulled aside the blue, checkered curtain hanging across the entrance and saw Bobby lying on his bunk reading a book. Bobby looked up a little surprised to see him.

"Can I come in?" asked Joey Dee.

Bobby sat up putting his bare feet on the concrete floor. "Yeah, sure, come on in," said Bobby clearly happy that Joey had come by. "Sit down," he said patting the foot end of the bed.

Joey walked in and sat down. "How come you didn't come to see me after work?"

Bobby looked a little surprised. He didn't expect Joey to want him to come by like he used to. "Oh, I...I..., to be honest, I guess I didn't think you wanted to see me so much anymore."

"Bobby, I still like you. I love you, in fact. You're like my brother. You can't stay away just because I won't have sex with you," complained Joey.

"Who said I wanted to have sex with you?" asked Bobby defensively. "I never ever said I wanted to have sex with you!" He exclaimed.

Joey sighed and said," Well, no, you never said you wanted to sleep with me. Not in so many words. But you're in love with me...I mean...like that...gay...and you kissed me."

Bobby hung his head and said, "Yeah, I love you. You made me realize that. But I'm not thinking about the sex, Joey."

"What else could you be thinking, Bobby?" Joey asked.

"I'm just feeling," answered Bobby looking up at him. "If I feel love for you and want to kiss you, that doesn't automatically translate into having sex with you," Bobby tried to explain.

"That makes no sense to me," said Joey clearly confused. "You kissed me and you've made it clear how you feel about me. That means sex is in there somewhere, doesn't it?"

Bobby inhaled deeply and exhaled slowly with his cheeks puffed out. "I don't know," he said finally. "I've never had sex with anyone, I mean, so, when I think about how I feel, I'm just not thinking about having sex with you."

"Jeez, Bobby," complained Joey. "That's even worse! You want me to be the first!"

Bobby didn't respond to Joey's accusation. He thought about it for a minute and realized that Joey Dee was right. He did want Joey, but Bobby really didn't know what that meant in real, practical terms. "It isn't that I want you to be the first," he finally said. "If sex is an extension of how I feel, then, OK, sex is in there somewhere. But it's fantasy and I know that. The thing is, though, I realize I've had crushes on guys all my life, and I'm just so used to denying myself and suppressing my feelings, that I don't think about the sex part very much. So you don't have to worry. I'm really OK with just a friendship. Honest."

Joey Dee looked at him closely. It made Bobby uncomfortable and he looked down again. "If you're anything like me, though, you'll always wish and hope that I'll come around," said Joey. "I'm always the eternal optimist who thinks that, with time, everyone will love me. You can't be like that, Bobby. I can't do that, so you'll be miserable all the time if we stay close, won't you?"

Bobby chuckled and said, "No, I won't." He looked up at Joey and continued, "You're my friend. That's all I want from you. You made it clear it can't be anything more, so I respect that. I'm done with it. You can't be paranoid that I'm going to sneak up on you and try to jump your bones."

"Fair enough," said Joey Dee. "Maybe I am being paranoid."

"You are," said Bobby. "So you aren't gay, OK. That's it. I get it. I can't change it. It would be crazy for me to keep hoping that you'll suddenly realize you're gay. So, let's just be friends and I promise you that's all there is."

"That means, that if I meet a girl, you won't interfere, right?" asked Joey. Bobby furrowed his brow at the question then thought about the fiasco with Lien and how unlikely it would be to meet another girl.

"What girl you gonna meet here?" asked Bobby smiling. "You're in fucking Vietnam! You think there's some hot chick behind every tree?" Then he chuckled out loud.

"I know. I know," said Joey trying not to smile. "Bobby, this is serious. C'mon, don't try to turn this into a joke, OK?"

"Joey Dee, you c'mon," said Bobby. "Lighten up. It is funny, y'know."

Joey pursed his lips trying not to laugh, but he broke down and smiled broadly. He reached up and shoved Bobby onto his back and said, "You shithead!"

Bobby spread his arms and legs and laughing said, "Come get it, Joey. It's all yours!"

Joey got up off the bed and walked to the doorway. "I tell you what. I'll ask around for ya and find another gay guy who'd be interested, OK?" asked Joey with a glint in his eye.

"No, don't do that!" said Bobby sitting up somewhat alarmed. "I'm not ready to advertise it yet."

"Then behave yourself," said Joey. "I'll come by in the morning before work, OK? We'll go to breakfast."

"Yeah, OK," responded Bobby. He stood up and walked towards Joey. "Joey, thanks for being my friend. I really am sorry about you and Lien. I know I didn't handle it right, but you've been great to me and I really appreciate it."

Joey put his arms around Bobby and gave him a hug. "Bobby, you are really like a brother to me. You hurt me, but I love you, so in the end I can forgive you, y'know? Can you understand?"

"I think so," said Bobby.

"Besides," added Joey. "You were right. I was acting stupid. Lien and I could never be together, I knew that, but I was so blissed out over her that I couldn't think clearly. Your friendship is more important to me. One day, maybe we'll go back to the States and we'll be able to see each other, talk on the phone, whatever. We just can't ever be together the way you want."

"Joey, forget that," said Bobby stepping back from him. "That's done and over. I don't know what's going to happen with me, but I can sort out my feelings enough to be friends with you without any problems."

Joey smiled and nodded. "Good, 'cause I want to talk to you about something I've had on my mind. Not tonight, though. Tomorrow, OK?"

"Sure," answered Bobby shrugging his shoulders wondering what it was about. "Tomorrow, then."

"G'night."

"G'night." And Joey left Bobby alone in his cubicle. He got undressed and crawled into bed. He lay there for a while thinking about what Joey could possibly want to talk about, but fell asleep without any problem.

Joey came by Bobby's at seven. He walked through the curtain and saw Bobby lying on his stomach only half covered by the white government issue sheet. Joey took one corner of the sheet and jerked it away from Bobby's body. He was totally nude, which surprised Joey. He had no idea Bobby slept in the nude. Bobby woke up, turned his head to see Joey Dee's expression of surprise.

"Damn, Joey Dee! I thought you didn't like guys!" said Bobby in his morning voice. He rolled over, grabbed the sheet from Joey's hands, covered himself and stood up.

"Get your ass in gear," ordered Joey. "I'm hungry."

"I'm up. Hold your horses. I'll be ready in fifteen minutes," said Bobby as he slipped into his olive drab boxers, grabbed his shaving kit and walked to the showers. Joey Dee decided to follow him and have the talk he had been planning.

"I need to talk to you, Bobby," said Joey Dee. "It's important."

"OK, so talk," Bobby said through a yawn. They walked together through the company, but Joey Dee couldn't seem to find the words to explain what he was thinking. Bobby realized it must be really important or Joey would have just opened up. He stopped, turned and asked, "Joey, what's up? What's so important?"

"You know, we've been here over three months now, right?" said Joey Dee as he began laying the groundwork for his news.

"Yeah..." responded Bobby.

"And, uh, we both think it's pretty miserable here," continued Joey Dee.

"That's an understatement," agreed Bobby.

"Well, I, uh, I'm going to extend my tour of duty and, uh, transfer to a different unit," said Joey Dee with a tone in his voice that made it clear he was relieved he had said it.

Bobby was so shocked he couldn't say anything. Instead he just stared at Joey.

"Say something, Bobby," Joey urged.

Bobby narrowed his eyes and turned his head slightly. He was both a little angry and very sad, but he wanted to sound upbeat and approving. "Oh...a transfer...so...have you already put in the paperwork?"

"No, not yet. I wanted to tell you first," said Joey.

That made Bobby feel slightly better, but he was still feeling very emotional. "There's no chance I could talk you out of it?" Bobby asked.

"I thought you might say that," said Joey. "But, no, I don't think so. I like the money I'm making here with the combat pay and I could save a bundle if I stayed. But you and I both know I couldn't stay here in this unit."

Bobby nodded his head, but didn't say anything. He started walking towards the showers again. "C'mon. I gotta take a shower and we gotta get to work," he said changing the subject.

Joey Dee followed him quietly for a while then asked, "Why don't you come with me?"

Bobby reached the door of the showers, stopped and said, "Come with you...you mean extend and apply for a transfer to the same new company."

"Yeah...that's what I mean," Joey said. "Let's do it, Bobby."

Bobby looked down at the ground shaking his head. "God, Joey, I can't make a decision like that right now. I'd have to really think about it," Bobby lamented.

"I know, and there's time to do that. I don't have to do this today, y'know," Joey responded as if a negotiation might work. "Think it over. We'll figure it out and if you don't think it's a good idea for you, then that's the way it'll be."

"But you're gonna do it no matter what?" asked Bobby.

Joey Dee nodded his head and began chewing on his lower lip. "I gotta do it,

Bobby. I just can't stand this place anymore and without Lien..."

Bobby opened the shower room door and walked in closing the door behind him. Joey Dee stood there in front of the door for a few seconds then followed him in. Bobby was already naked and walking into the shower stall. Joey walked to the shower stall and leaned against the wall next to the entrance. He heard Bobby turn on the water and step under the shower. "I was thinking about Cam Ranh Bay, Nha Trang or Qui Nhon," yelled Joey so that Bobby could hear him in the shower.

Bobby stopped washing and yelled back, "You mean for the transfer?"

"Yeah...the transfer," Joey shouted. "They're on the beach, too, but they were actually French resort cities. I figured they'd be more like a tropical vacation!"

"Man, you are an optimist," Bobby shouted. "Either that, or you're just stupidly naive."

"Ah, come on, Bobby, don't bust my balls about this, OK?" Joey said.

Bobby finished showering, turned the water off, grabbed his towel hanging on a nail and wrapped it around his waist. He came out of the shower stall, stopped in front of Joey still leaning against the wall. "I'll shave really quick so we can get a little food before work," he said. "I'll think it over and we'll talk about it later."

Joey Dee nodded his head in agreement. "I'll meet you at the mess hall," he said and walked towards the door. He opened the door, but before he left he turned and asked, "I know this is gonna sound strange to you, but, if you really love me like you say you do, why would you ever say no?"

Joey's words stung Bobby. He leaned over the sink like he was looking in the mirror, and didn't turn around. Those were exactly the emotions he was dealing with and Joey Dee's question sounded more like a manipulation than anything sincere. He decided he wouldn't answer the question. "I'll be at breakfast in a couple minutes, Joey. Save a place at the table for me."

Joey looked a little sheepish and was about to say something when a dark-haired young man, muscled, handsome and wrapped in a towel pushed past him through the door. He glanced quickly at Joey then continued walking to the sinks. He put his shaving kit up next to Bobby's, turned on the water and began washing his face. Bobby looked quickly at him and was taken aback at how handsome he was. He looked over his shoulder at Joey Dee who smiled, raised his eyebrows and indicated with a nod of his head that the handsome guy next to him might be interesting. Bobby's eyes widened, then his eyebrows narrowed slightly and he shook his head no. The dark-haired man turned and looked at him and Bobby quickly turned his head back to the mirror. The man then turned his head to look at Joey Dee still standing in the doorway looking back at them. He turned back around, opened his shaving kit and pulled out shaving cream and a razor. He glanced quickly out of the corner of his eye at Bobby, but Bobby pretended not to notice. Bobby hadn't seen him before in the company, and he wasn't a traffic analyst or he would recognize him. Either he didn't work the same shift in ops or he worked somewhere else.

"The name's Brad Williams," he said without looking away from his reflection in the mirror.

Bobby glanced quickly at him, turned back to his mirror and said, "Bobby Pinks."

"Traffic analyst?" Brad asked.

"Yeah, and you?" Bobby responded with as much nonchalance as possible.

"Naw, linguist," he said. "Just got here this week."

"Oh," Bobby said but couldn't think of anything else to say.

Brad paused briefly, looked again at Joey who was still standing at the door. He began fussing again with his shaving cream and razor then said quickly, trying to sound friendly and casual, "You know, you should come over to my hootch for a cocktail. I'd like to get to know some of you guys in the company better."

Bobby nearly dropped his razor and Joey Dee's jaw dropped. Neither had expected any such invitation, especially with the word 'cocktail' in it. They both understood the word instantly as a euphemism for something else.

"I'll see you later, Bobby," said Joey and he left quickly closing the door behind him.

"Yeah, OK," Bobby responded obviously confused. He was staring at Brad and still holding the razor, but he hadn't resumed shaving.

Brad watched him for a moment then, smiling, said, "You know, you're supposed to use the blade on that razor to take off the beard. Or did you have something else in mind?"

Bobby was slightly embarrassed and quickly continued shaving.

"Well?" asked Brad directly and with expectation.

"What?" Bobby asked looking at Brad's dark brown eyes for the first time.

"Would you like to come over to my hootch sometime?" Brad asked again.

"Oh, sure..." said Bobby without conviction, then with a little more clarity and resolve repeated with a nod of his head, "Sure...yes...definitely."

Brad smiled and said, "Good." He finished shaving, put his razor back in the shaving kit, took off the towel and hung it up on a nail outside of the shower room. Bobby couldn't stop staring at him. Brad stopped at the doorway into the showers, turned around to show Bobby a full frontal view of his nakedness and said, "I work mostly days. I'm in C Hootch. Any time after dinner would be fine." He turned around and walked into the showers.

Bobby's heart was pounding after seeing Brad in all his glory. He rinsed his face, towel dried it, grabbed his stuff and ran back to his hootch. When he pulled back his blue-checkered curtain, Joey Dee was sitting on the bed waiting.

"I thought you were going to breakfast," said Bobby entering the cubicle.

Joey Dee chuckled and said, "Well, I had to find out what that was all about back there. Cocktails anyone?" he asked mocking Bobby.

"Oh, come on," moaned Bobby. "Does everything have to be sexual with you?"

"Cocktails, Bobby?" he asked again. "You're in fucking Vietnam in a goddamned makeshift shower. Who the hell is going to invite you over for cocktails?"

"I don't know," Bobby said with an uncertainty and slight whine. "Maybe it was just his way of being friendly," he said opening his eyes a little wider to make the point.

"Are you serious?" asked Joey Dee with both concern and surprise. "This isn't an act, right? You're really that naive?"

Bobby shook his head and admitted, "No, I know. He said cocktails. What else could he mean except..."

"Except his dick," Joey Dee finished Bobby's thought for him.

The thought crossed Bobby's mind like a revelation and then laughing he said,

"Yeah! His dick! Wow! You should've seen it!"

"You saw his dick?" Joey Dee asked with surprise.

"Yeah, he took off his towel and walked towards the showers, but turned around and showed me everything he's got," explained Bobby still laughing.

Joey Dee started to laugh, too, and fell back on the bunk. He stretched his arms up and put his hands behind his head. "Could be true love!"

"Shut the fuck up," Bobby said. "I didn't say I was going over there."

Joey Dee sat up quickly and asked, "You told him no?"

"Well, no, not exactly," said Bobby blushing slightly.

"You told him yes! Oh, fuck! Bobby's gonna get laid by some hunk in the showers, tsk tsk," mocked Joey Dee shaking his finger at him. "You could lose your security clearance over this one. Man, this is better than me and Lien!"

"Joey, come on, nothin's gonna happen," said Bobby.

"Oh? You don't want anything to happen?" asked Joey.

Bobby didn't answer as he pulled his underwear then fatigue pants on, fastened the brass belt buckle and slipped a t-shirt over his head. Finally, he said, "Actually, he's really cute, isn't he? If he's really gay, and I get to know him better, maybe then..."

"Oh, OK," said Joey Dee nodding his head, clearly not convinced. "Once you get to know him better. Who do you think you're foolin'? You don't want to be a virgin anymore. Man, we're all desperate. Don't tell me that shit. If you got the chance, you'd do it in a New York minute!"

"Ok, so that brings up something else here," said Bobby feeling confident and firm in himself. "You said in the showers that if I loved you the way I said I did, I'd transfer with you. What kind of duplicitous bullshit is that?"

Now Joey Dee looked a little embarrassed and looked down but didn't say anything.

"You just trying to manipulate me or what?" asked Bobby.

Joey Dee stood up and said, "Yeah, you know, I'm sorry. I shouldn't have laid that on you. I'm used to you, Bobby, and I don't want to be here in Vietnam without you. You make it bearable for me. That's all. Yeah, I guess I was being manipulative."

Joey finished dressing and put his jungle hat on. "OK, as long as I know. Let's go get breakfast." They walked out of the hootch together.

They really didn't talk much about it at breakfast. They ate quickly and headed for work. Bobby was feeling very confused. He felt that Joey was toying with him. He kept thinking about Joey not being gay, yet he was asking Bobby to be with him, even transfer to a new company together. Bobby was suspicious, but at the same time he had a little glimmer of hope that burned in his brain. He thought back to Joey's comment about being the eternal optimist and how Bobby might keep that little flame of desire for him ablaze if they were to stay close friends. Well, Bobby began feeling that optimism. He started hoping again. He worked all day in operations, but was preoccupied thinking about extending and transferring. He argued with himself about it. Why would he even consider staying in Vietnam beyond his required one year? Love would be about the only thing that might push him to extend, but if Joey weren't in love with him, then what would be the point? Why couldn't they just go back to the States together? At least there would be enough opportunity and diversion there for Bobby to make his own life, find a lover or partner, and still be friends with Joey. He thought about Brad in the showers. Joey Dee was right, that he'd be risking his security clearance. In Vietnam, there would be little chance for Bobby to develop an emotional relationship outside of his friendship with Joey. With that realization, there was only one answer to Joey's suggestion: Bobby couldn't stay.

Bobby quietly and privately came to this decision as he was working to find certain patterns of code in some North Vietnamese Army communications that had been copied and put in his inbox. He circled groups of letters that fit a pattern, initialed the sheet of paper and filed it in a basket to be taken to decoding. He noticed quite a large stack of messages—many more than usual. He stood up to stretch and realized it was already 02:10pm. He sat back down, took a new stack of papers and just as he started, the Commanding Officer came in the operations room. Bobby stood up at attention and waited. The C.O. had very seldom come into Ops, so when he did, Bobby knew it had to be important.


## Changing States—Changing Minds

"At ease, men," commanded the C.O. "You all can sit down." Bobby looked around and there were a few other guys in the room who took their seats. Bobby kept his eyes on the C.O. and sat in his chair. Another group of traffic analysts came in and they stood around the room against the walls. Bobby knew something was up, but he couldn't imagine what it was.

"Men," began the C.O. "The North Vietnamese have gone into a massive communications change. Now, you all haven't experienced anything like this before and I have to warn you that the work ahead of us will be difficult. Our intelligence gathering efforts have to start all over from scratch, in order to recover the networks that have been changed. And you can read that as lost."

As the realization hit him that they had no idea any more what call-signs or what frequencies the North Vietnamese were using to communicate, Bobby also understood that life in Da Nang would become even more miserable. He listened to the C.O. explain in more detail what was happening, but it was all a blur. He was thinking about Joey and wondered if those in the other operations area had been told yet. There was a time offered for the analysts to ask questions, but no one raised his hand. The C.O., apparently finished with his news, stood at attention, which signaled the men in the room to stand again. Bobby snapped to attention. The C.O. said, "At ease!" Men began to file out of the room and Bobby returned to his chair. He took his stack of papers, shuffled through them, and thought to himself that these most recent messages must contain very important information. He doubled his efforts to find important patterns in the letter groupings and was concentrating so hard on it that he didn't notice Joey Dee come in and stand next to him.

Joey reached down and touched him on the shoulder. Bobby looked up and smiled. "So you know about the communications change, too?"

"Yeah," Joey said nodding his head. "I've already been given new instructions and I'm being assigned over here with you guys."

Bobby looked at him raising his eyebrows. "How come?"

"There's a group of new guys coming in and, ah, they're going to put the more experienced traffic analysts with them, so there's not enough room over there for me," Joey Dee answered.

"Makes sense," Bobby said. "Well, you might as well find a chair and make space for yourself at this desk here."

"Well, Todd Churchill is coming over, too," said Joey. "He's actually been doing the same work as you, so it'd be better if he sat here."

"Whatever," said Bobby. "Jensen over there is working on a similar network as you. You can sit at his desk then." Joey looked in the direction Bobby indicated, but there was no one there. Jensen was on sick call that day. He walked over to the desk and began looking at the bulletin board.

Todd Churchill walked in carrying a large box of office supplies. He stopped in the doorway and Bobby pointed to the end of his desk indicating a place for it. Todd came in and set it down.

Bobby said, "You can get a chair from the other room. I think there's an extra one in there."

Todd walked out without saying anything. Bobby looked at him closely for the first time. He didn't know him well. He was one of those young men who had a very rugged masculinity and a slight swagger to his walk. There was a macho quality to his appearance and demeanor. His dark brown hair was cut to regulation and, although clean-shaven, a shadow was already appearing on his cheeks, even though he had shaved before coming to work. When Todd came back carrying the chair, Bobby expected to get into a conversation. But Todd sat down, turned the chair with his back to Bobby and he started sorting out his office supplies.

Bobby looked at Joey Dee, furrowed his brow in annoyance and indicated by facial gesture that he didn't understand Todd's behavior. Joey Dee shrugged his shoulders and raised his arms with palms up to show Bobby he had no idea what Todd's problem was.

"Bobby, I'm going to go back, clean out my desk and bring my supplies over. I'll be back in a few minutes," said Joey Dee. Bobby nodded his head and went back to work.

After a minute without any words between them, Bobby interrupted the silence. "So, Todd, um, you wanna see what we've been working on here?" asked Bobby.

Without turning around, Todd said, "Naw, I'll have someone else show me."

Bobby was disturbed by his attitude and asked, "What's the problem? I'm here, I know just as much as anyone in the room."

Todd turned around then and, leaning forward, quietly said, "Yeah, but you're the only faggot in here." He turned back around and shuffled through his supply box.

Bobby was stunned and scared. With hands shaking and his voice quivering he managed to ask, "And where would you get an idea like that?"

"Joey Dee told me how you came on to him and tried to kiss him," said Todd with clear hatred in his voice. "So you just keep to your faggot self and don't talk to me, OK?"

Bobby collapsed on the inside. He was so hurt and angry that he couldn't sit there any longer. It was the first time anyone had ever confronted him with being gay. He got up and quickly made his way to the restrooms. He washed his face with cold water, dried off and looked at himself in the mirror. He felt betrayed and alone. He felt hatred and he wanted to hurt Todd and Joey Dee, but mostly he wanted to hide himself and wail in grief. He pulled himself together and walked back to his bay. When he walked in, Joey Dee was at his new desk unloading his office supplies from a large cardboard box. Bobby didn't know what to do or what to say. He wanted to lay into Joey Dee and let him know what he thought, but with Todd in the room and being at work, he decided he'd say nothing for now and confront Joey Dee later. He sat down at his desk and went back to work, but he was fuming.

Joey Dee stood up and walked over to Bobby after he had finished unpacking his box and arranging his desk. Bobby wouldn't look up.

"Bobby?" Joey Dee said trying to get his attention. Still Bobby didn't respond. He wanted to, but he was afraid his anger would overtake him and he would create a scene. He kept quiet and continued working on his traffic. Joey Dee grimaced and tightened the left corner of his mouth as he tried to figure out why Bobby wasn't answering. He reached down and touched his shoulder saying, "Bobby, did you hear me?"

Bobby gently moved his shoulder out from under Joey Dee's hand, put his pencil down, stood up and walked out without looking at him. Joey Dee was completely perplexed. His gaze followed Bobby out of the room. He turned to Todd and asked, "What the fuck's wrong with him?"

Continuing to look at his traffic and without looking up he said, "Aw, he's prob'ly all pissed off, 'cause I called him a faggot."

Joey Dee looked horrified. "You did what?"

Todd turned around and complained, "Hey. He was trying to sound all superior and shit, wanting to explain to me what they were working on here. I just told him to keep to his faggot self and not to talk to me."

Joey Dee shook his head and rolled his eyes in disbelief. "You know, Todd, you're an asshole. What'd ya wanna go and say somethin' like that for?"

Todd looked disinterested, but responded, "Hey, man, you're the one who told me he was a faggot, so what the fuck do you care if I put him in his place?"

"'Cause I care, that's why!" Joey Dee exclaimed with some irritation. "What else did you say to him anyway?"

"I just told him that you told me he came on to you, that's all," Todd answered.

Joey Dee panicked. Now he understood Bobby's reaction. "You stupid mother fucker!" yelled Joey Dee. Then with concern someone would hear him he softened his voice into a whisper and said, "OK, he tried to kiss me and I didn't like that, but he IS my friend and I don't give a shit if he's gay!"

Todd turned back around to his work and said, "Get out of my face, Joey Dee. You and your faggot friends can just fuckin' stay away from me, OK? Shit, you're as bad as he is, if you still hang out with him!"

Joey Dee was really furious. "Fuck you, Todd!" he said with anger and walked out with the intent of finding Bobby. He walked down the hallway towards the administrative office area. Bobby came around the corner and they nearly bumped into each other.

"Bobby, are you OK?" Joey Dee asked with concern.

Bobby just glared at him and smiled, but it was a smile filled with disdain. "You told Todd," he said almost whispering so that his voice didn't carry down the hallway.

"I know, I'm sorry," admitted Joey Dee quietly. "I told him the day after it happened on the beach, but we were just talking and I was a little confused, Bobby. I asked Todd what he thought about it. I had no idea he'd be such an asshole about it."

"What were you doing?" Bobby asked accusingly. "You tell this guy I kissed you and you think, what, he's going to sit down and get into a philosophical discussion about it?"

Joey Dee sighed deeply. "I wasn't thinking, OK? It was stupid, I know. But we can just get past this, can't we?"

Bobby looked down and asked, "You're being honest with me? You really don't care that I'm gay?"

"Bobby, I've told you a hundred times I don't care," Joey Dee said with sincerity. "I feel bad I let that out to Todd. I didn't know he was such an asshole."

Bobby nodded his head and said, "OK. I can get past this, I guess, but you gotta tell me if anyone else knows about this."

"I don't know if Todd has said anything to anyone, but he's the only guy I talked to about it," Joey Dee said.

Just then an officer came down the hall towards them. They both stood at attention and saluted as he walked by. The officer looked at them quizzically and saluted back.

"Come on, we'd better get back to work," said Bobby.

"Yeah, it's almost four," Joey Dee said looking at his watch. "Did you look at the schedule?"

"We're working until six today," answered Bobby.

"Shit. We gotta sit in ops with Todd for another two hours?" Joey Dee asked.

"Well, we don't have to talk to him," Bobby said and they walked back to the bay. Bobby was feeling better realizing that, although Joey Dee had told Todd about the kiss, he didn't tell him out of malice or revenge. Maybe this would all work out in the end after all.

"Not today, maybe, but what about tomorrow and the day after that?" asked Joey Dee. "He wasn't exactly happy I called him a mother fucker."

Bobby looked surprised and chuckled. "You really called him a mother fucker?"

Joey Dee glanced at Bobby and started to laugh. "Shit. I really called him a mother fucker. He's gonna kill me!"

"I'll be your bodyguard," laughed Bobby.

As they walked into the bay, Todd glanced up at them but didn't say anything and continued working. Joey Dee and Bobby went to their respective chairs and started working without saying anything further. Every now and then they'd glance at Todd, look at each other and smile. The two hours passed rather quickly and, although Todd didn't say anything else about it, they all felt the tension between them. Captain Lennox, the operations officer, came in and relieved them at six. The next crew took their positions for their twelve-hour shift and Bobby, Joey Dee, and Todd all left for the mess hall. Bobby and Joey Dee walked a little more slowly than Todd and lagged a good ten yards behind—just far enough that he couldn't hear their conversation. In the mess hall, Todd completely ignored them and it seemed he wasn't in the mood for any further confrontation.

Joey and Bobby got their dinner and sat down together. Joey Dee watched Bobby as he put salt and pepper on his food. Bobby could feel Joey's gaze like a breeze coming through an open door. He looked up.

"What?" he asked.

"I'm just wondering, if you made a decision about the transfer," Joey said.

Bobby paused, looked at him then started eating. After he swallowed his first bite, he said, "Yeah. I've decided. I can't do it. I wanna go back to the States where I can have a social life, maybe find a boyfriend, get out of the Army and go back to school or something."

"If you stayed, you could save a lot of money for school," suggested Joey.

Bobby looked closely at him. He set his knife and fork down, pushed his plate forward and intertwined his fingers together. "Joey Dee, if you want to be with me, even if just as a friend, then, think, how am I supposed to get along here with you? I have no chance for any kind of personal life beyond our friendship."

"Well, I don't either!" Joey exclaimed. "What, just because I met Lien, you think I'm going to just come on to any pretty Vietnamese girl here and it'll work? Shit, you'd interfere with any girl I met, anyway. You know you would."

"That's not fair, Joey," Bobby complained. "I wouldn't. But that's not the point. That's all hypothetical. You and I are not. And you would undermine any relationship I might get into with another guy. You already brought up the fact that I'd lose my clearance, if it got out that I was having sex with another G.I. So, I know you would always be thinking about it and looking for it."

Joey Dee realized that Bobby was probably right. He didn't admit it out loud, but he knew the truth of it. He took his water glass and drank from it. He was starting to feel nervous and uncomfortable with this friendship. Bobby noticed the agitated expression on his Joey's face.

"What's the problem?" he asked.

"No problem," Joey answered shaking his head. Bobby was unconvinced.

"What are you thinking about?" he asked.

Joey Dee looked down at the table and said, "I'm trying to understand myself, why I want you to stay with me here. Why I need you..." he stopped talking and drank his water empty.

Bobby rolled his eyes a little, chuckled and asked, "What are you trying to tell me, that you're gay after all?"

"No, I'm not trying to say that. I mean...I can't help it. I don't understand my feelings for you. It's like I can't imagine my life without you in it and I've never felt that way before about anyone. I mean, anyone outside of my family."

"So, you're nervous that it might be a sign you really are gay?" asked Bobby intrigued.

"Fuck, I don't know what I'm saying or what I mean," said Joey with some frustration. "I've never ever thought about sex with another guy. I've never thought about sex with you. It's just the emotions I have and what I feel about you that weirds me out."

Bobby leaned forward and placed his hand on top of Joey's. "It's OK. It's really

OK to feel that way about someone," he said trying to comfort Joey. "Especially me! I want you to feel that way about me and not just because I'm in love with you, but because we're friends here."

It struck Joey wrong to hear Bobby say again that he was in love with him. Joey stood up quickly and said, "God, Bobby, can't we just stop talking about all this? It's just bullshit, y'know? Fuck, can't you just let it go?"

Before Bobby could respond, Brad Williams walked in. He immediately noticed Bobby and Joey Dee and walked towards their table. Bobby watched him from the moment he came into the mess hall. Joey picked up his tray and empty glass and said, "Looks like you got company. See ya tomorrow."

"Joey Dee, wait up, huh?" Bobby said. "Let me get rid of him and we'll go back to the hootch together."

"Bobby, you got a chance with this guy, I think. Why waste it on me? Go for it, huh?" Joey said, turned around and walked away.

Brad arrived at the table and watched as Joey walked away across the mess hall. "Does he have a problem with me?" he asked.

"Joey Dee? No, no, he doesn't have a problem with you," Bobby said gesturing with his hand to the seat next to him. "Sit down."

"Thanks," Brad said sitting down and scooting the chair closer to the table. "Well, I'm just wondering because that's the second time he's left when I've come in."

"Just coincidence, Brad," Bobby assured him. "He's working through something, but it doesn't have anything to do with you."

"OK, if you're sure it's not about me," said Brad.

"I'm sure," answered Bobby. "So, where you from in the States?" he asked changing the subject.

"California. Monterey, actually, and you?" Brad asked.

Bobby chuckled thinking about California. Brad looked 'California.' He was one of those good-looking, bronzed Adonises Bobby noticed in magazines and commercials. He felt really provincial and unsophisticated in comparison. "Bismarck, North Dakota," Bobby said looking directly at Brad to see his reaction.

"Far out!" he said. "What a place to come from!"

"Well, obviously, it's not California, but it has its own charm," Bobby answered honestly.

Brad bit his lower lip and nodded. "Must be kind of idyllic and pastoral," he said smiling.

Bobby looked at him closely wondering about those words idyllic and pastoral. Why would this guy use words like that? It made Bobby a little worried that maybe his use of 'cocktail' was in the same vein; namely, it was just Brad's way of talking and there was nothing behind it—no euphemism implied. Bobby just suddenly blurted out, "Were you coming on to me in the showers?" He even surprised himself that his internal censor didn't catch that question before he expressed it.

Brad looked directly at him and smiled. "And if I was?" he asked.

"Nothing. I just wanted to know for sure," said Bobby.

"Ok, yeah, I was sort of coming on to you," he answered truthfully.

"What made you feel it was OK to do that with me?" asked Bobby.

"I don't know, just the way you were staring at me...the whole thing with the guy in the doorway..." he stopped his thought.

"Joey Dee," said Bobby.

"Yeah. Anyway, I thought you were attractive and you seemed interested in me, so I thought I'd ask, y'know?" he said in a low voice, but not a whisper.

"You don't seem to be nervous about it or like you're hiding it," observed Bobby.

"Oh...right...the pervert thing," Brad said with cynicism.

"I wasn't implying you're a pervert!" Bobby explained quickly.

"Well, yes, you were on some level or you wouldn't have phrased it the way you did." Brad said.

"Then I was calling myself a pervert, too," Bobby said.

"Well, you might be," said Brad with a glint in his eye. "So you are queer."

Bobby nodded, "Yeah, I'm queer. At least I think I am anyway."

"Do you get any action around here?" asked Brad.

"You mean sex?" Bobby asked naively.

Brad laughed and said, "Yes. I mean sex. You guys get it on together here?"

"No...or at least I'm not aware of...ah...guys doin' each other," Bobby said with some discomfort.

Brad looked directly at Bobby and said, "Maybe you and I could change that."

That embarrassed Bobby and he said, "I don't know. Maybe after I get to know you better."

"Oh, cool. A real romantic," Brad said patronizing him. "I didn't think gay guys were much into that scene."

"Scene?" asked Bobby.

"Yeah, right. I forgot. You're from Bismarck," Brad said rudely and laughed.

"Look, if you're going to make fun of me, then there isn't much chance that we'll ever even become friends," said Bobby clearly perturbed.

"Sorry," Brad said sincerely. "I can be a jerk. I didn't mean anything by it." There was a moment of silence between them before Brad suddenly spoke up. "So, you in love with this guy—Joey Dee?"

Bobby didn't want to answer the question so he stood up, put his hands on his tray and said, "Listen, um, it's getting late and I have some letters to write yet this evening, so I'll catch you later, OK?"

"I did it again, huh?" asked Brad. "Sorry, it's none of my business."

"I really do have to go," said Bobby.

"Can I walk with you back to your hootch?" Brad asked.

Bobby was a little surprised at the request, but he didn't see anything wrong with it. "Sure, I don't mind, I guess."

"Far out!" exclaimed Brad as he pushed his chair back and stood up. Bobby took his tray to the return window and met Brad at the door. Todd walked by just as Brad and Bobby were about to leave.

"Faggots!" he said quietly as he walked by on his way to the return window. Brad grimaced slightly and Bobby just followed Todd with a piercing gaze. They turned around and left the mess hall walking into the darkness of the very humid, tropical night. The compound was kept fairly dark with only the dim glow of the lights visible from the various hootches that were lining the walkways. Between the hootches themselves there was only the blackness of night and anything in that space was invisible to the eyes on the walkways. As Brad and Bobby walked through the center of the compound, Brad said, "So, that guy must know you pretty well."

"Not really," Bobby answered. "He just thinks he knows me. All he knows is that I tried to kiss Joey Dee. I don't know. He might be trouble."

Brad grabbed Bobby's hand and pulled him into the darkness between two hootches. He pushed Bobby back against the side of a hootch, leaned over and kissed him deeply and passionately. Bobby melted into the warmth of Brad's body. He put his arms around his shoulders and pulled him even closer. Brad broke the kiss and whispered, "So, Bobby, did you kiss him like this?"

Bobby didn't answer. He broke away from his embrace and went back to the dim light of the walkway. Brad emerged out of the darkness smiling and said, "See ya later, OK?" Bobby didn't say anything and Brad walked off into the night. Bobby went in the direction of his hootch, but didn't get too far when he heard a dull thud, a scream, then yelling and swearing. The screaming voice sounded like Brad, so he ran towards the sound. He couldn't see well, so he slowed down and quietly called for Brad. Suddenly he heard groaning off to the right. He stepped off the dimly lit wooden walkway into the darkness and shadows and nearly stumbled over Brad's body. He knelt down and touched him.

"Brad? Is that you? Are you OK? What happened?" he asked each question without a break in his voice.

"Oh, I hurt. Damn! These guys came out of the dark and attacked me. Called me faggot and beat on me," he said with effort and a heavy voice.

"Oh my god!" Bobby exclaimed with anger. His jaw was clenched and his hands formed into fists. "I can't believe someone would do this! Let me get you up and back to your hootch, OK? Can you walk, you think?"

"Yeah, I'm OK," groaned Brad. "Help me up, huh?"

Bobby helped him to his feet, put an arm around him and helped him walk to his hootch. "Who would do that—just assault you for no reason? Fuck! How do they know you're gay, anyway?" asked Bobby.

"I don't know, maybe they were watching us back there and I was the one who came their way. Otherwise it would've been you, I guess," theorized Brad.

"I bet it was that asshole, Todd!" growled Bobby.

"You know, I don't think so," Brad responded remembering his attackers. "Todd's a pretty big guy. There were three of them, I think, and none of 'em sounded like Todd's voice. They weren't as big, either. I don't know, maybe he was one of 'em, but I don't think so."

"Well, I wouldn't put it past him, y' know? He's got a real thing about queers and he was really mean and vulgar to me in ops the other day," Bobby explained.

"So what? Why would he come after me? You think, just 'cause he saw me with you in the mess hall?" Brad asked with doubt in his voice.

"I don't know, maybe. But then again, he doesn't seem to be, you know, a racist or bigot or something like that, so maybe he just hates queers," offered Bobby.

"Naw, all that shit is wrapped up into one mean attitude—niggers, kikes and faggots. You know the type," Brad said with disgust.

"Yeah, unfortunately," answered Bobby. "Ok, here. Let me get you inside to your cubicle." Bobby opened the door, led Brad to his cubicle and gently lowered him onto the bed. He turned the light on and took a good look at him. His face wasn't puffy, bleeding or black and blue, but he did have a bump on his head.

"So, you don't look so bad," said Bobby optimistically.

"You mean my face? They didn't get me there. I was able to block their blows with my arms. They hit my head, shoulders and torso," Brad said unbuttoning his shirt. Bobby reached down and helped him remove the fatigue shirt and his t-shirt. Bobby noticed right a way that his chest and upper back were very red and turning black and blue.

"Yeah, looks like you might be sore for the next few days," Bobby said examining Brad's body. "You're gonna report this, right?"

"Naw, I don't think so," said Brad looking up towards the ceiling.

"What!? Why not?" asked Bobby with concern.

"Bobby, it won't help. I can't identify anyone and if I reported this, the whole fucking company would look at me differently. There's no investigation gonna happen, even if I went to the C.O. Things just don't work that way," Brad said sadly and honestly.

Bobby thought about it for a moment, nodded his head, pursed his lips then said, "It's bullshit, but you're probably right."

"Hey, I got some liniment and some Aspercreme in my footlocker. Get it for me, huh? I'll put some on and just lie here and read for a while," Brad said.

Bobby opened the footlocker, searched through the toiletries and pulled out both a little bottle of liniment and the tube of Aspercreme. He handed them to Brad and said, "I can stay here with you if you need me to. I got nothin' better to do."

"Thanks, but I'll be OK. You can go. You don't have to stay," Brad said looking directly into Bobby's eyes.

The directness of his stare made Bobby a little uncomfortable. He put his hands in his pockets and responded, "If you're sure you're OK. I'll see you tomorrow, OK?"

"Sure. See you tomorrow," Brad answered nodding his head. Bobby turned and walked out of the cubicle then outside. He was a little nervous that those guys might come after him, too. He walked briskly back to his hootch but he met no one on the walkway.

He got undressed and flopped onto his bunk. He lay there staring at the ceiling thinking about Brad, the kiss, Joey Dee and even a thought about the problem at work raced through his mind. He had to admit that he loved the kiss, but he was still in love with Joey. He was also intrigued by the developments in operations. Just as life in Da Nang was finally getting interesting, Joey Dee wanted to go somewhere else. He fell asleep only to be awakened by the sound of sirens, thuds and explosions. Another rocket attack. Bobby was experienced enough now that he had become philosophical about death. If he were meant to die, the rocket would land on him, whether he was in a trench or in his bed. He decided to roll off the bunk onto the floor and crawl under the bed. He reached up, grabbed the blanket and pillow and made himself comfortable there on the floor. He adjusted the pillow and fell back asleep. He slept there until morning.

Joey Dee came as usual to wake Bobby up. He walked into the cubicle and saw that Bobby wasn't in bed. He stopped, gathered his thoughts and tried to figure out where Bobby could be, especially since there was no blanket or pillow there. He just happened to look down and he saw the sole of Bobby's left foot in the shadows under the bunk. He got on his hands and knees to look. "Bobby, what the fuck are you doing sleeping under your bunk?"

Bobby woke up to see Joey Dee looking at him on all fours. He smiled and said, "I didn't want to run out to the trenches during the attack last night, so I just rolled under here and went back to sleep."

"You're a real dumb shit sometimes, you know that?" Joey Dee said with a certain humor in his voice. He stood up and Bobby slid out from under the bunk.

"Well, I'm still alive, so I wasn't all that dumb now was I?" he said playing a little one–upmanship.

"Come on, let's get to ops. I heard some rumors this morning from the night shift. I wanna get in there and find out what's goin' on," Joey Dee said with anticipation.

"Joey, wait! I gotta tell you about what happened last night!" Bobby said somewhat frantically.

"Tell me later, Bobby, shit's comin' down in ops and we gotta get in there," Joey Dee said with impatience. "Go on ahead then," said Bobby with some frustration. "I'll catch up."

Joey Dee left the hootch and walked quickly to the operations center. He showed his badge to the security guard at the gate and entered the compound. The ops building was a relatively large one-story concrete structure without windows that housed the intelligence gathering efforts for the area called II Corps (two corps). There was a large main hallway and four bays or wings that extended out from both sides of the main hall. At each end of the hallway there was a large office area. The command and executive officers did their administrative work at one end and the cryptographers worked at the other end. Neither of these areas was accessible to anyone except for those with a need to know. One had to have a certain degree of top-secret clearance to enter especially the crypto area. The traffic analysts worked in bays seven and eight at the very end. The linguists were in six and the Morse code operators, who copied the encrypted messages, occupied the remaining bays. Joey walked down the hall until he reached Bay 7. When he walked in, every analyst was intensely focused on a pile of copied messages. There was a chalkboard with a schematic drawing of a communication's network, but there were no longer any frequencies or call–signs on the board. Everything had been wiped clean.

Todd Churchill had come in a few minutes before and had already started going through his stack of encoded messages. Joey Dee stopped by his desk and asked, "So, what's the news? I heard this morning at breakfast that Central Communications Hanoi went silent. Do you know anything?"

Todd looked up shaking his head. "No, haven't heard anything yet, but the increase in messages is overwhelming, so something serious is going on. If CenComm Hanoi went down, then we're in trouble."

Joey Dee nodded his head and moved on to his desk. CenComm Hanoi was the source of all communications to North Vietnamese and Viet Cong units inside South Vietnam. If they went silent, there would be no chance of reconstructing the network to gain the necessary intelligence for U.S. troops. He looked in his in-box and there were at least twenty messages in there. He took the stack, sat down, unlocked his drawer and took out his key. The 'key' was a large book of previously discovered patterns of letters and numbers that the cryptographers had managed to decode. He had become familiar enough with the patterns that he didn't have to refer to it much anymore. He just knew from continuous use, which patterns were identifiable and which were still unidentified. As he glanced through the messages, it dawned on him that he didn't recognize a single grouping of letters or numbers. Nothing looked familiar. He rolled back in his chair and swiveled to face Todd across the room. "Hey, Todd," he said. "Are you finding anything in your messages that's in the key?"

Todd looked up and shook his head no. "Nada, nichts, nichevo," he answered. "It's almost spooky."

Bobby came into the bay at that moment and Joey Dee said, "Bobby, you gotta look at this shit. I got nothin' but shit-bees with nothing recognizable in 'em."

Todd looked at Bobby quickly, made a face and turned away. Bobby noticed his behavior but didn't address it. He avoided walking near Todd, going all the way around the room to get to Joey Dee.

"Well, if they're all shit-bees, at least you know the Morse code was sent by hand," said Bobby briefly defining the term 'shit-bee' as the vernacular version of 'XB', the term used for any unidentifiable Morse communication sent by a hand key. "What are the frequencies and call-signs?" he asked.

"They're listed here, but there's not a single frequency I've ever seen before and the call-signs don't look at all like CenComm or any of its outstations," said Bobby looking through one message after the other.

Bobby grabbed his own stack of messages from his in-box and, shuffling through them, came to the same realization—nothing was recognizable. He sat down in his chair, placed his papers on the desk and leaned back. He was thinking about what it could mean, but he had no previous experience with this sort of thing, so he couldn't fully grasp the significance of it. Out of the corner of his eye he noticed someone come into the bay. He turned to look at the door and it was Brad. His eyebrows arched and he sat up in his chair as Brad made eye contact and started walking towards him.

"Hey, guys," Brad greeted the room. "I have a partial translation of a message that was intercepted day before yesterday. I thought you'd all like to see it. It's still a little questionable, because the crypts could only break it in some places. But what they have, we were able to translate. We can fill in the gaps with logical assumptions, which is always risky, but it's still pretty amazing. Take a look."

He handed Bobby the paper and Bobby read it with genuine interest. Bobby briefly looked up at Brad, made eye contact, but didn't say anything. He looked back at the paper and it appeared to be saying there was a massive attack being planned in II Corps for the following week. There was no specific location mentioned or at least that part hadn't been decoded. Bobby got up, walked to Joey and handed him the message. Joey read it and then handed it to Todd. Todd passed it on to Phil Jensen. After everyone there read the message, Joey Dee asked Brad, "Do you guys think it means an attack on Da Nang?"

"We're not sure," Brad answered. "But we're damned lucky we got that out of it. It helps, actually, because the crypts are finding some repetition that should lead to more plain text copy. We should have some more translated by this afternoon. We're hoping there's more specific info in it. We've already forwarded this to command, so we should be hearing soon what they plan to do."

"But if we can't piece together the new network, we'll have no way of really knowing where they plan on attacking," said Todd.

"Right," agreed Brad looking at Todd with a piercing gaze. "The ditty-boppers are searching the bandwidths for anything that even sounds vaguely similar to the guys they've been copying in the old nets."

Bobby walked towards Brad and said, "there's not much we analysts can do, is there? The ditty-boppers have good ears for this shit and if they can't ID the transmitters and senders, then Charlie will be able to pull off any attack he wants. We won't know where he is."

"No, we won't," Brad agreed. "Looks like we'll be moving permanently to the trenches."

Bobby knew what Brad meant. They could look forward to a long period of Red Alert, which required everyone who wasn't at work to be in the trenches and on guard duty. Bobby looked directly at Brad and noticed that his entire demeanor had changed. He was behaving like a real soldier—responsible, concerned and determined. He wasn't at all the seductive, fickle playboy he had been the night before. Bobby had momentarily forgotten where he was and was about to open his mouth and say something personal, when the Commanding Officer walked into the bay. All the men stood at attention and saluted. The C.O. returned the salute and said, "At ease."

The men stood at ease and listened.

"I've decided to go on Red Alert beginning at twelve hundred hours today," he said. "You'll be putting on full gear after lunch and you'll have to wear helmets and flak jackets even at your desks. After work, report to the trenches and the bunkers, where you'll be given C-Rations from now on for dinner. Unfortunately, men, you'll be spending the first night in the trenches, but tomorrow night you'll take the bunkers. You and the linguists will rotate with the ditty-boppers."

Brad looked at Bobby and smiled when he heard that the linguists and analysts would be together during the alert. Bobby smiled back, but wondered what sort of change had come over Brad. He wasn't acting like the jerk he had been.

The C.O. looked around at the men in the bay and finished by saying, "You'll be kept informed of any new developments that might affect you. I can't impress upon you enough how volatile this situation is right now. We are looking at a complete communications change in Hanoi and the possibility of a full-scale attack on II Corps installations. That means this place here and all of us. Good luck." And he turned around and left.

"I'd better get back to work," said Brad.

"Will you have lunch with me?" Bobby asked. "I want to talk to you, OK?"

Joey Dee looked up quizzically at Bobby, but didn't say anything.

Todd smirked then said with disdain, "Hey, lingie, you need to watch out for that one. I hear tell he likes boys."

Bobby turned around quickly and with controlled anger said, "Shut the fuck up, Todd. Mind your own fucking business, OK? No one wants to hear your bullshit."

Todd swiveled in his chair facing Bobby. "You think a cock suckin' fairy like you can shut me up? Why don't you come over here and try it?"

Brad stepped forward in between Todd and Bobby and said, "You two need to kiss and make up or find girl friends!"

Joey Dee started chuckling and said, "I'd love to see that. Todd kissing Bobby! Man, that'd be better than any porn!"

Todd got up, grabbed his hat in anger and walking to the entrance of the bay said, "You mother fuckers are perverted, man. I'm outa here." And he left.

Bobby faced Brad and commented, "You look OK this morning. How do you feel?"

"Mmm, not too bad, but it still hurts a little," he said glancing at Joey Dee.

"What hurts?" asked Joey Dee with some curiosity.

"That's what I wanted to tell you about!" exclaimed Bobby nearly whispering. "Let's talk about this at lunch, huh?" He motioned with his head towards Phil Jensen who was sitting at his position and only now and then overhearing the conversation.

"Sure. Later, then. I'll come by when I leave for the mess hall. But do me a favor and don't invite that Todd guy! He's a bummer, man."

"Oh, it goes deeper than bummer, believe me," said Bobby rolling his eyes and shaking his head. "OK, I'll wait here until you come by." Brad turned and left the bay.

"What's all that about?" asked Joey Dee.

"Nothing," said Bobby widening his eyes and looking towards Phil Jensen. "He was just acting a little weird before and I want to know what he was up to."

"What do you mean weird?" asked Joey.

Bobby leaned towards his ear and in a near whisper said, "Well, let's just say he had his hands all over me last night and he was really trying to come on strong, but I played it maybe a little too cool and he left me standing in front of the hootch. Then someone came out of the dark and beat the shit out of him! I found him and took him back to his hootch."

"What, you're shittin' me! You mean he is gay and interested in you and then someone pounded him?" asked Joey Dee in complete surprise.

"Come out in the hall, I'll explain it all," Bobby whispered.

Once out of the bay, Bobby said in all seriousness, "I think he's gay, but I don't really know if he's interested in me. He's just horny and it sounded like he was looking for some 'action' as he called it," Bobby said.

"So what do you want to talk to him about? It sounds like you have him figured out," remarked Joey.

"I just want to find out if that's really what he was up to...you know...trying to get me to do that with him," said Bobby.

Joey smiled knowingly at Bobby and said, "Well, whaddya know! You gotta keep me updated, OK? But who would've attacked him and why?"

Bobby's face showed the sadness and concern he had for Brad. "He thinks three guys did it. They called him a faggot and then laid into him."

"Holy fuck! Is he reporting it?" asked Joey Dee.

"No, he says it won't help and it might just make things even worse," Bobby said with frustration. "He's probably right."

"Wow, that's heavy," said Joey Dee shaking his head. "Bobby, you gotta be careful. It's clearly not all that safe in this company for you."

"I know," said Bobby thinking about the possibilities. "But I'm not going to let it stop me or bother me too much."

"You know I'll help if you need it," offered Joey Dee.

"Oh, believe me, you'll be the first person I call, if I need help!" Bobby said accepting the offer.

"Look, I think I'm gonna go down the hall and talk to the ditty-boppers," Joey Dee said. "I wanna know what they're thinking about all this commchange stuff. I'll be back before lunch."

Bobby nodded and walked back into the bay. He sat down at his position and started going through his traffic again.

Todd came back into the bay and asked out loud, "So, who's this linguist? I've never seen him before," asked Todd.

Bobby answered without looking at Todd, "Some new linguist named Brad. That's all we know. We met him yesterday."

Phil Jensen, who had been sitting at his desk watching and listening to the earlier confrontation between Bobby and Todd, finally spoke up contributing more information. "I heard guys talking about some new linguist whose dad is a Brigadier General. Williams I think they said his name was. Was that the guy?"

"I don't know anything about his dad, but he told me his name is Brad Williams," Bobby answered. Now he was really intrigued. If Brad's father was a Brigadier General, then his behavior was all the more bizarre and Brad was a lot more complicated than imaginable.

Suddenly, in the distance they heard the familiar shriek of an incoming mortar or rocket. Everyone, conditioned by these intrusions, fell instantly to the floor and took cover under the desks. There was a muffled thud and a brief quake, then silence. The sirens went off sounding the attack. Todd, Phil and Bobby ran out of the bay through the emergency exit to the sandbag bunker outside. Another whistling sound and another thud, this time accompanied by an explosion. The round hit more closely than the previous one. Brad, three other linguists and Joey Dee came running into the bunker and crouched down along the sides. More whistling and more explosions, two more, three more, then nothing. They waited in their crouched positions looking up as if they could see the sky above the bunker. The all clear sounded and there was a collective sigh of relief.

They stood up, filed out of the bunker and went back into the ops building. They wondered where the rounds hit. It was pretty close wherever it was. They all went back to work without saying much. It was quiet time. After attacks like this, everyone became much quieter for a while.

At 11:45am, Brad came into the analysts' bay and stood in the doorway holding his olive green jungle hat in his hands. Bobby looked up and Brad raised his eyebrows indicating he was ready to go to lunch. Bobby nodded his head without saying anything, put his desk in order and joined Brad at the doorway. They both left without saying anything to anyone. Joey Dee watched them leave and it made him uncomfortable. Seeing them together gave him an unsettled feeling. He felt alone—maybe a little abandoned. He decided he would go back to his hootch to get his helmet, flak jacket and M-16 before going to the mess hall, just in case of another attack.

"OK, that's it for me for a while," announced Joey Dee. "I'm gonna get some lunch. I'll see you guys later." And he left ops. Walking back through the company to his hootch he couldn't help but think about Brad and Bobby together. He became worried that Bobby would get together with Brad and then not transfer with him to another company. He knew he had no hold on Bobby. His own words rejecting Bobby's advances echoed in his head. Yet, he needed Bobby. He was dependent on him and he wasn't ready to let him go.

After getting his gear from the hooch, he walked into the mess hall and surveyed the room looking for Bobby. Bobby saw him first, looked his way but didn't react to his presence. Brad was talking to him and he wanted to concentrate on what he was saying. Joey Dee finally found them sitting at a table in the middle of the mess hall. They had plates of food and seemed to be lost in discussion. He grabbed a plate and stepped in the chow line.

"Yes, my dad's a general. He's the commander at the base in Wiesbaden, Germany," he said taking a fork full of food.

"So, that explains why you were so official and military at work, then," Bobby remarked. "Your behavior last night with me was pretty forward and bordered on being rude. Today, you're the model soldier. It was just very weird for me."

Brad hung his head and said, "Look, I told you I can be a jerk sometimes. I was just showing off. You made it clear you haven't fucked around much and I thought you'd be an easy target. I'm sorry 'bout that. But then I got the idea that you were into Joey Dee and, ah, it seems to me you guys got something going between you and I...I guess, I don't want to interfere."

Bobby smiled slightly, chuckled a bit and said, "Well, we're friends, but that's all. Joey Dee's straight."

Brad moved his head from side to side, narrowed his eyes and scraped his upper lip with his lower teeth. "You guys don't act like you're just friends. Everyone thinks you're in love with each other."

"What do you mean everyone?" asked Bobby somewhat alarmed.

"Guys talk, Bobby," Brad said directly. "I heard that guy named Todd's been saying shit about it."

Bobby rolled his eyes and said, "Todd's an asshole. Joey Dee made the mistake of telling him that I tried to kiss him on the beach. He's been giving us grief ever since. He called me a faggot and won't talk to me. It's ridiculous."

"Oh yeah, you mentioned it last night. You tried to kiss him but he's straight?" asked Brad somewhat surprised.

"Yeah, unfortunately," said Bobby with a sigh. "It didn't go over very well. I don't know. It just came over me and I leaned over and kissed him, like it was the most natural thing in the world. Joey Dee nearly came unglued, but it hasn't really affected our friendship. He's just adamant that he's not gay and that there's no way he's ever gonna kiss me back."

"Well, that's his loss," said Brad smiling affectionately at Bobby.

"You starting that shit again?" asked Bobby

"What shit?"

"That seduction smile—the flattery—like last night," Bobby answered.

"Bobby, I'm not gonna lie. I'm attracted to you. I'm just putting it out there and you can do with it what you like," Brad said with his customary casualness and savoir faire. "You know what you want, and you know what you can't have. You have to decide."

"OK, and what if you...we...get caught?" asked Bobby.

"You mean, because of our clearances and the military bullshit...?" Brad asked.

"Yeah, the Army!" Bobby responded emphatically. "We are in the Army and it's against the military code of conduct."

"So is smoking weed and screwing prostitutes, but that doesn't seem to stop anyone," Brad said rationalizing his behavior. "Look, they know all of us G.I.'s do this crap. They know about the whores, the drugs, they know that some guys are suckin' each others' dicks. They know! You just can't shove it in their faces, that's all. A little discretion goes a long way with these people. Believe me, I've grown up in the Army. I'm an Army brat. I know how it works."

Bobby noticed Joey Dee dressed in his combat gear pulling a chair out from a table near the doors. He sat down and without looking up started eating. Bobby felt a little guilty that he wasn't having lunch with him. He wished Joey would just come over to the table and join them. Somehow things were changing between them. They suddenly weren't talking to each other like they used to. He looked up at Brad and realized that because of him, everything was beginning to change for Bobby. He was feeling this need or desire to move towards Brad, primarily because it meant the possibility of finally ending his status as a virgin, and with someone who apparently had some experience. Yet, he sensed that, in spite of Joey Dee's expressed openness about it, it wouldn't be a welcome development and Joey would be hurt.

"I'm done," said Bobby. "I'm gonna get my gear and head back to ops. I want to talk to Joey for a minute, too, so I'll see you later, OK?"

"Sure," Brad answered. "No problem. Hey, that, ah, invitation still stands, you know. Any time after dinner. My place." Brad smiled at Bobby and shrugged his shoulders.

Bobby smiled and said, "Thanks. I'll think about it." And he walked over to Joey's table.

"Joey, you could've joined us, you know. You didn't have to sit here by yourself," said Bobby.

"I didn't know how personal your conversation was, so, I didn't think I should," Joey answered. "If you were planning some secret rendezvous, I didn't want to know about it, y'know?"

Bobby sat down and said, "Come on, Joey. You don't have to act like you're walking on eggshells around me. It's just not like that."

Joey looked right at Bobby and asked, "Are you going to get together with him?"

"I don't know, Joey," said Bobby honestly. "Not right now, anyway." Bobby started to smile and then continued, "I'm not over you yet, so, he'd be getting me on the rebound. No future in it for him, y'know."

"He didn't give me the impression he was looking to get married, if you know what I mean," Joey said with a little disdain in his voice.

"Now who's jealous?" asked Bobby.

Joey snapped his head upwards and said, "Fuck you, Bobby. I don't need that."

"Oh, so now suddenly, mister open-minded gets to have it both ways. You get to fall in love and I'm not supposed to be jealous. But when I might be lookin' at someone else, you can be jealous and I'm not supposed to say anything. That's bullshit, Joey, and you know it. Besides, you're straight, remember? Why do you care?"

Joey Dee looked down and said quietly, "I don't know, Bobby. I don't know. I shouldn't care. It shouldn't bother me, but it does. I'm afraid of losing you...to him."

"God, Joey, don't say that. Don't do this to me!" lamented Bobby. "Do you realize how much you're jerkin' me around here? How much you're fucking with my mind? You're acting just like you're in love, but you say you're not. You love me like a brother, right? But you're stringing me along holding me close, then at the same time keeping me at arm's length. It makes me crazy!"

Bobby waited for Joey to say something, to react in some way, but Joey just sat with his head down looking forlorn and distant. Bobby got up and said, "I have to get my gear. I'll see you back at ops. Think about it, Joey." And he left the mess hall. Joey sat for a couple of minutes thinking about his relationship with Bobby. He didn't know what he felt. He didn't know if he was capable of loving him romantically, but he did know that he was scared of it. It was fear, just fear that kept him in this morbid state. Something had to change. He got up and headed back to ops.


## There Are No Heroes

Operations was a beehive of activity. The ditty-boppers were frantically copying every message on every frequency they could find. The T.A.s were pushing their red pencils over message after message, circling any probable or possible combinations that might lead the crypts to a breakthrough in the code. The crypts were up to their necks in code to be broken and the lingies were speeding through translations of Vietnamese cleartext. The administration officers were running from bay to bay checking on progress and reporting hourly on the developments. By the time it came to shift change, mounds of work had been accomplished and yet nothing resolved. This CenComm communications change created a massive gap in U.S. tactical intelligence and with the little bits of knowledge gleaned over the last couple days, things looked very ominous. The mission at hand was critical and urgent. The entire network had to be recovered in order to gain any usable intelligence. It was as if you woke up one morning, turned on the television and all the stations were gone, or at least nothing was on the channel it was supposed to be. As you hit the remote you found all the station call signs had changed as well. The networks had different call letters and channels, and the cable stations were all mixed up. The only way you could identify who was what and where was to channel surf until you recognized a television personality associated with a particular program on a particular station. Then slowly, through trial and error, you could reconstruct a TV guide that was usable. This is what these intelligence workers faced, except multiply the possible number of frequencies and call signs at least by ten to get an idea of the magnitude of the problem.

Swing shift came in all dressed ready for combat and the day shift moved out into the trenches and bunkers. Bobby, Joey, Brad and the rest of the linguists and analysts went into the trenches that surrounded the company. They set up their guard sites and machine gun bays and got ready for a very long night. A jeep pulled around about 06:30pm and unloaded the C-rations for the night. Not usually a welcome sight, but the men were so hungry by then, it didn't matter what they ate.

It was dark by 8:00pm and the men found individual spaces to nest in. Bobby, Joey and Brad stayed close together and created space to lie down and sleep for the night. Todd and Phil were also close by. They were all grateful it wasn't raining. Both Brad and Joey were assigned to guard duty on the machine guns between midnight and 02:00am. Bobby and Todd had guard at the same time, but facing the other way with just an M-16. They tried to get some sleep before midnight, but all the men just lay there in the darkness thinking about the events of the day and problem-solving in their heads for work. Bobby dozed off for a while and was wakened by the Sergeant of the Guard about 11:45pm. He rolled over and whispered to Joey Dee, "Hey, Joey, you awake?"

"Yeah. I don't think I fell asleep at all," Joey responded.

"I didn't either," piped in Brad. "Well, let's get up and get this over with."

Bobby felt a little intimidated having to stand guard next to Todd, although Todd hadn't said another word about being gay since the incident in operations and the mess hall. Bobby felt a little emboldened by that fact and also that there was another gay man around. He decided to talk to Todd to find out whether anything had changed. He still wondered, too, if Todd had gay-bashed Brad. He thought, if the conversation went OK, maybe he'd ask.

"So, Todd, I hope you can handle pulling guard duty with me," Bobby said as casually as possible.

Todd looked at him then, looking away, said, "Yeah, I guess I'll be OK."

"I'm really not a bad guy, y'know," added Bobby.

Todd smiled and said, "I'm not either. I just don't understand the faggot thing."

"Well, I don't understand it either. It's just something that happens inside me and I don't seem to have any control over it," Bobby revealed.

Todd looked at him, pushed out his lower lip and asked, "But you don't want to be like that?"

"At first, I didn't, no," Bobby answered. "But my heart and my dick seem to be connected somehow and I fall in love just like you do. I just fall in love with other men. I'd rather fall in love than not, so at this point I guess it is what it is."

"It seems you're settling for less," suggested Todd. "Maybe therapy or something would help."

Bobby laughed quietly. "OK, maybe I need therapy. But, even if that's true, you know, lots of straight guys might need therapy, too, but no one would deny them their humanity or tell them they weren't allowed to fall in love anyway."

Todd thought for a moment about Bobby's assertion and said, "You have a point, but it still doesn't seem right to me."

"I'd be lying, if I said it didn't scare me," admitted Bobby, hoping a small show of vulnerability might disarm Todd. "I could be bashed by some redneck or arrested or get a dishonorable discharge or lose my job on the outside. They'd print my name in the paper as a pervert. All of that scares the shit out of me."

"But you still do it, why?" asked Todd.

"Well, I'm not doing anything, but let me ask you, why do you come on to women? Why do you want sex?" asked Bobby.

Todd laughed and shook his head. "What kind of a question is that? That's like asking why grass grows or why birds lay eggs. It's just what men do. It's just what I do," Todd said.

"Exactly," said Bobby. "And I'm no different. I just get a hard-on for other men. But it's just what I do. It's just what's inside me."

Todd looked at Bobby, twitched his nose and scratched his temple. "See, that's what freaks me out, Bobby," Todd admitted. "It makes me nervous to be around you."

Bobby glanced at Todd and realized that, on some level, Todd both wanted Bobby to be turned on to him and yet was terrified of the possibility. "Todd, I'm not attracted to every man I see, any more than every woman you see gets you goin'. I'm not going to come on to you, just because you have a dick."

"You don't like me?" asked Todd very directly.

"Todd, what do you think? You were rude and mean to me. No, I don't find that particularly attractive," Bobby said somewhat perturbed with equal directness and honesty. "You're safe."

"No, I meant...me...you don't like me. You're not attracted to me," Todd said again slightly insulted, but trying hard not to let that come through his voice.

"That's what I'm sayin', Todd," Bobby reiterated his point, staying away from the whole of idea of attraction. "As a person, you have some work to do. How am I supposed to like you, if you aren't civil to me? I think you're a fuckin' bully."

Todd went silent again. Bobby looked at him in the darkness. He could tell by the expression on his face, even in the dark, that Todd's feelings were hurt. That surprised Bobby. Todd was human after all. Bobby felt a little remorse for calling him a bully.

"Hey, I didn't mean it so harshly, y'know? I just don't know you very well and you came across as a bully. I didn't mean to hurt your feelings," Bobby said with some sincerity.

Todd looked out into the night and didn't respond. Bobby decided to let him think it over for a while. After a few minutes of silence, Bobby said, "Maybe you could think back to when you called me a faggot and realize how that felt for me. I got scared and not just of you. It scared me to have you sound like you hated me so much."

Todd turned his head and looked briefly at Bobby then looked straight ahead. "I did mean it when I said that," he said clearly reflecting on his own attitudes. "You aren't supposed to be in the Army. You remember, you told them when you took your oath that you weren't a homosexual. You lied to them, right?"

Bobby understood the question and he had even thought about the same thing. He had, indeed, answered that he was not a homosexual. At that moment in time, he could honestly say he was not a homosexual. He wasn't any sexuality of any kind.

Neither homo- nor hetero-. He was a virgin. He said quietly, "No, I don't think I lied. I really wasn't a homosexual then. Or actually I didn't know I was a homosexual then. I didn't find that out until I met Joey Dee."

"How could you not know?" Todd asked with genuine curiosity.

Bobby thought about the question for a moment and realized he, of course, had known deep down that he liked men. "You're right," Bobby answered. "I suppose I did know...sort of...on some level. I knew I was different. I knew I liked being around guys, but I didn't know about the love thing until a few months ago. I knew about faggots and queers, but I thought they were perverts and really scary. That's why I was so disturbed when you called me that. But I really didn't consciously know all of that was inside of me. Deep down, though, sure, I guess I did know that I liked guys."

"What I mean is, the first time you had sex with a guy, you had to know you were a queer," Todd explained with confusion in his voice.

"Oh," Bobby said in response, then just stopped.

"What?" asked Todd.

"I've never had sex with a guy," Bobby admitted shuffling his feet a little. He was uncomfortable admitting that to Todd.

"Wait! You've never had sex with a guy, but you say you're a homosexual?" Todd asked clearly perplexed.

"That's just it," Bobby said. "I would like to have sex with someone, but I'm a virgin. I just know that I was really into Joey Dee until he made it clear that he wasn't into me that way. So, my feelings are definitely homosexual, but that's all I got at this point."

"Wow, that's far out," Todd exclaimed. "What if you don't like it? I mean, you like Joey Dee, but what if you had sex with some guy and you really hated it. What if you're really into women?"

Bobby was stunned by the question. He hadn't really considered it. Once he kissed Joey Dee and became aware of his feelings for him, he just assumed he was gay. He never thought about the possibility that he could feel that way about a woman.

"I don't know. I...I don't know," Bobby said tentatively. "I've never been in love with a girl, so I don't know how to answer your question. But, I could turn it around and ask you the same thing. What if you had sex with a guy and liked it? What if you're really gay?"

Todd withdrew into himself in response to the question. It startled him. He had never thought about it. He didn't have an answer for it. The confusion he felt was unsettling. Out of the confusion, however, came a moment of clarity. He and Bobby had carried on a civil conversation. They were talking about sex and really communicating.

"I just know," Todd finally said almost in a whisper.

"And just knowing that, how does that make you feel about yourself?" Bobby asked with sincerity.

"What do you mean?" Todd wasn't sure what Bobby wanted to hear.

"Well, I just know, too," Bobby said with confidence. "And when I kissed Joey Dee? It felt good and right, and it was the most natural thing in the world for me. How does it feel to touch a woman or kiss her?"

"Right. It feels like that. Like you said," Todd said nodding his head.

"And that's all I'm sayin', Todd," Bobby explained. "You gotta go with what feels right. You can't really do anything else."

"No, y'can't. I can't anyway," Todd agreed.

"That's all there is to it," Bobby stated and then leaned against the trench wall and waited for Todd to think about it all. After a few minutes of silence, Bobby thought it would be the right time to ask about the attack on Brad.

"So, do you hate me so much that you would just pound on me for no other reason, if you had the chance?" probed Bobby.

Todd looked at Bobby and didn't say anything for a moment.

"It's an easy question," Bobby said becoming concerned at his silence. "Yes or no."

"No," Todd answered abruptly. "But I know what you're thinkin'. You think I kicked the shit out of Brad, don't you?"

Bobby raised his eyebrows and looked at him with growing animosity. "You know about it then?" asked Bobby.

"Yeah, I heard," Todd said in a lower tone of voice and looking down.

"Did you do that?" asked Bobby with a less accusatory tone.

Brad turned his head towards Bobby and said, "No, I didn't. I know who did, but I wasn't one of 'em. I heard 'em talking and laughing about it. Fuckin' idiots, if you ask me."

"Why didn't you report it?" asked Bobby this time with more accusation in his voice.

Todd answered defensively, "I could ask you the same thing. Why didn't you report it when you found out?"

"Brad said he didn't want to draw attention to it. He didn't think anything would be done about it anyway," Bobby answered.

"Yeah, he's probably right. It was just none of my business and I tried to forget what I heard," admitted Todd. "You believe me then?"

Bobby was a little surprised that Todd would even be concerned about what he thought or believed. "Yeah, I guess so." Bobby looked closely at him and continued, "I'm glad you didn't do it. I don't know how I would've reacted, if you had said you were part of it."

"Look, I don't really hate you. Or Brad. I don't. To be honest, you guys are the first gays I've ever really known about and it just freaked me out, that's all. But I wouldn't..." Todd paused to find the right words. "...I wouldn't attack someone or hurt someone for it. Especially in my own company. That's not me. That's not what we're doin' here."

Bobby smiled. The military code of honor was at play here. They were in the same unit and the unit cohesion was paramount for Todd. Black, white, gay, straight, whatever, if they were all in the same unit, they were all equal in Todd's eyes. No man left out, no man left behind. That was The Law. Nothing more needed to be said at that point. They stood in complete silence for the rest of their guard shift. When their shift was over they went to sleep. Bobby fell asleep hoping that he had made a friend out of Todd. Todd drifted off thinking that Bobby had a self-confidence that he himself didn't have. Bobby knew better who he was and Todd wasn't nearly so sure. He was glad he wasn't a homosexual, but he also envied Bobby's confidence. The night passed without incident and the sun rose the next morning revealing a bluish mist hovering over the ground. The mountains behind Da Nang seemed to rise up out of the mist and as the sunlight hit them, they turned deep purple, then rose, then a brilliant gold. Swing shift had crawled into the trenches about 01:00am and those men were now getting up in shifts to replace the different guard stations along the trench. The day shift crawled out of the trenches and went to clean up for their turn in operations.

Everything had become so intensely focused on the communications change and the crisis at work, that Joey Dee and Bobby didn't have time to deal with their personal problems. It was all they could do to maintain the hectic work schedule under the circumstances. There simply wasn't enough mental or emotional energy left by the end of the day to discuss their feelings. They happily slept in the bunkers every other night and unhappily moved into the trenches when they had to. This went on for four days and by the end of the fourth day, knowing they had to go back into the trench, simply ruined their good humor and destroyed their mood. As they settled in the trench for the night, each in his self-selected nest, Brad rolled over towards Bobby and whispered, "I could use being tucked in for the night. Interested?"

"I'm not going to have sex with you out here in the trench, Brad, if that's what you're after," said Bobby clearly indicating he was disgusted by the suggestion.

"I'm not saying, we should have sex," Brad said, "I'm merely asking to be tucked in."

"And what would I do to tuck you in then?" asked Bobby.

"What are you guys whispering about over there?" asked Joey Dee.

"Nothing, Joey, we're just talking," Bobby answered.

"We're not just talking," admitted Brad. "I want a good night kiss, but he won't."

"God, you two, get some sleep, huh?" ordered Joey Dee.

Brad started laughing and Bobby rolled over and pulled his blanket up over his head. Suddenly, the familiar whistling of an incoming rocket pierced the night air and the concussion and explosion that followed lit up the night sky. Everyone jumped up, they grabbed their weapons and peeked over the ridge of the trench. The rocket landed squarely in the middle of the company, but did not hit anything directly. Then another whistle was heard, another and another, and all the ear could hear was the sharp whistles and then concussion and explosion after concussion and explosion of the incoming rockets. They seemed to land all around the company compound and then building after building exploded and went up in flames. On the horizon, the men could see that there was a general attack underway all over Da Nang. Explosions and fires lit up the horizon and it seemed that all of the U.S. bases in the Da Nang area were under heavy attack. This was the dreaded offensive hinted at in the translated message Brad had showed them a week earlier.

In the distance, there was a different sound other than rockets. Firearms were being discharged. Machine guns. Joey and Bobby looked out towards the western perimeter and saw orange-red and green tracers blazing through the darkness. Charlie was conducting a ground assault on the compound!

"Holy fuck!" exclaimed Joey Dee. "That ain't just rockets. They're coming through the perimeter!"

The Sergeant of the Guard came running through the trench screaming orders at the men. "Man the machine guns! Everyone take firing positions and look out carefully. Shoot to kill anything that moves out there. There shouldn't be any American soldier out there right now, so if you see anything move, you kill it! Understood?"

"Yes, Sergeant!" responded all the men within ear shot. And then he moved on down the trench to repeat the orders to all the others.

Joey, Brad and Bobby lined up along the trench, their weapons resting on the ground and their eyes looking through the sights. Todd, Phil and the others were on the machine guns. Bobby's hands were shaking and Joey was so scared he could hardly breathe. Brad kept adjusting the strap on his M-16 and wrapping it around his arm. He leaned over to Bobby, and with his free hand pulled him gently towards his face. He leaned forward and kissed him, his tongue probing between Bobby's teeth deep into his mouth. Bobby didn't resist.

"Listen!" exclaimed Joey Dee. "The rockets stopped!"

Brad broke away from Bobby and said, "Yeah, they've softened us up for the ground attack."

Bobby just stared at Brad after he stopped kissing him. Brad noticed and said, "Bobby, keep your eyes out there, OK? Those slippery little bastards can sneak right by you and you won't even know it, until they slit your throat."

"Nice thought," said Bobby and turned his eyes forward. "Maybe I should be looking behind me then."

About twenty-five yards down the trench to the right there was suddenly yelling and rifles began blazing their red tracers into the blackness. Flares were launched and there in the middle of the company compound were four Vietnamese in black silk pajamas, carrying weapons and running as fast as they could. Todd and Phil let loose in their direction with the machine gun. Joey, Bobby and Brad put their M-16s on automatic and sprayed the area in front of them until their magazines of ammo were empty and they had to reload. Everyone was so terrified, it was difficult to lock the new magazine in its bay and reload. It seemed to take forever to lock and load. No one could tell if the four VC had been killed or not. Even if they had, how many more were out there?

None of the men in the trench waited for flares or orders to do anything. They kept a constant barrage of machine gun and automatic weapons fire aimed at the center of the company compound until the Sergeant of the Guard came running through yelling, "Cease fire!"

They all stopped shooting, but kept their fingers on the trigger. Now there was yelling, screaming and weapons fire somewhere in the trench to the left. No one knew quite what to do at this point, except watch the red tracers fill the blackness of the night. Suddenly behind them, outside of the perimeter, a ground flare was tripped. They whipped around aiming their weapons into the eery light of the small flare. They saw nothing as the light of the flare dimmed then left them staring into blackness.

Todd leaned over to Bobby and whispered, "You think there's VC out there?"

Bobby nodded his head yes, but didn't say anything. His eyes were straining to see into the night. "See if we can get a starlight scope," suggested Bobby.

Todd thought over the suggestion for a second, then immediately ran down the trench to the Sergeant of the Guard. He had to be very careful as he hurried through the trench not to step on people or fall down. He nearly ran into the Sergeant of the Guard in the darkness, when he got to the trench command center. A little out of breath he asked, "Sarge, can we get a starlight scope? I think we got VC comin' in the wire!"

The Sarge reached into a large box on the ground, pulled out the scope and handed it to Brad. "You guys got a field radio down there?" he asked with concern.

"I really don't know, Sarge," Todd answered. "Who would have it, if we had one?"

"I don't know," he answered flatly. "Ask around, huh? Someone has to have one down there!"

Todd turned on his heels and hurried back to his position. "Here!" he exclaimed handing the starlight scope to Bobby. "Have you ever looked through one before?" he asked.

"Yeah, in basic training," Bobby answered quietly. "Let's see what we can see..."

He lifted the scope to his eyes and looked out into the darkness beyond the perimeter wire. At first he didn't see anything, but then he saw shadows moving—not left to right, but forward towards the trenches. "We need machine guns and flares aimed this way!" he exclaimed with urgency. "Hey, you guys, open fire over here! Todd get some flares!"

There was a box of flares a few feet away and as he reached in to get some he could see something else next to them. He knelt down and felt it—it was a field phone! He grabbed two handfuls of flares and passed them out to a few guys standing along the trench wall and said, "We got a field phone here, too, in case we need to call in."

"OK, guys, you got the flares. Now two at a time, shoot 'em off!" Bobby commanded. The flares went up lighting up fifty yards in front of the perimeter. The men could see the VC hit the ground as soon as the flares lit up. Without any further command, all the men on the line started shooting in the direction of the movement in front of them. Grenades were tossed, claymore mines exploded and the streaming, undulating lines of orange-red tracers on the bullets fired from the M-14s, M-16s and machine guns created a surrealistic work of art in the dim light. Finally, they all heard what sounded like the thunder of a herd of buffalo. On the horizon, a row of lights appeared and as they grew closer, the familiar shape of the Cobra attack helicopter became recognizable. They paused directly overhead, reared back and let loose with the earsplitting sound of rockets launched from their underbellies. The rounds landed in the area just outside the western perimeter and they continued the barrage for at least five minutes. They finally stopped and in perfect formation flew forwards toward the perimeter, then let loose again with a volley of rockets.

Another series of flares was launched, and in the brightness, the men in the trench could see hundreds of Vietnamese running through the company compound trying to escape the light and the cobra rockets. No one on the line waited for orders to fire, the entire line along the trench opened up. This time Bobby could see the dark moving shadows collapse as they were strafed by the bullets. He began screaming and cursing the VC and firing his weapon like a mad man. More flares, more gunfire, more bodies falling. Someone delivered more canisters of ammo and there seemed to be no end to the weapons fire, the red tracers, the explosions and the yelling. Suddenly, it all went quiet and there was only darkness and the heavy breathing of the men.

Bobby's knees were so weak, that he couldn't stand up anymore. He stepped back from the trench wall and collapsed onto his rear end. His hands were still shaking and his teeth were chattering like it was the middle of winter. Brad knelt down next to him and asked, "You all right, Bobby?"

"Yeah, I'm OK," Bobby answered still breathing heavily. "I just needed to sit down a minute."

Brad sat down next to him and put his arm around his shoulders. Bobby leaned his head against his chest and closed his eyes.

There was total silence for what seemed like hours, but really was only ten minutes. The men stood perfectly still the entire time waiting for something else to happen. The all-clear siren sounded, there was a collective sigh of relief, and the men began milling around again in the trench checking on each other, giggling nervously and feeling very relieved. Bobby reached up and took his helmet off, turned his face into Brad's chest and started to weep—not cry out loud or sob—just weep silently. Brad took his own helmet off and held Bobby until his shivering stopped. Joey Dee knelt down next to them and said, "How you guys doin'?"

"I think we're OK," Brad said. "Just need to let some of the tension out a little bit, y'know?"

"Yeah, I know," said Joey. Brad reached up and took off Joey's helmet, put his arm around the back of his neck, pulled him closer and kissed him. Joey Dee tensed and resisted momentarily, then acquiesced. He felt like he was melting away. He could feel Brad's masculine, square jaw and the facial hair around his mouth. The kiss was a revelation, but it didn't incite any eroticism. It was like therapy. Brad could feel the tension flow out of Joey Dee's body and when he was completely relaxed, Brad let go.

"Sorry, man," Brad said sincerely. "But I think we both needed that."

Joey didn't know what to say or do. He was thinking about the kiss and trying to understand why Brad did it. It wasn't a sexual thing. It dawned on him that Brad saw in him the need to stay very connected after the intensity of the fire fight. After the kiss he really did feel less stressed and more relaxed. His internal defenses and rigid self-protection he had raised in response to the attack had simply dissolved. He took his helmet, stood up and put it back on. Then he said, "Maybe. But I think I know what you were trying to do. So, thanks for making the effort."

"Hey, not a problem," Brad said with a lightness in his voice. "You're worth it."

"Bobby?" Joey said.

"Yeah?" responded Bobby as he sat up again.

"I think this lingie here is one of the good guys, y'know?" Joey Dee said with a wink.

Bobby looked up at Brad's face then back at Joey. "Yeah, I think he is, too."

Joey Dee extended his hand to Brad and they wrapped their hands around each other's wrists. Bobby stood up and Joey helped Brad up off the floor of the trench.

Todd Churchill came over to the three of them and asked, "Everybody OK here?"

"Yeah, I think we're all OK, thanks," said Brad. "How 'bout yourself?"

"Oh, my knees are still a little weak, and once I change my shorts, I'll be fine," he said joking.

All four chuckled and Todd reached over and lightly slugged Bobby on the shoulder. He looked a little embarrassed about it, but said, "I think you single handedly took out 'bout half o' those zips, Bobby," exclaimed Todd. "I don't know if you could see in the flares, but it seemed like every time I saw you shooting, those zips got blown away."

Joey Dee wasn't sure where Todd was going with the comment, so just in case he was about to attack Bobby again, Joey jumped in saying, "I thought that was you shooting like a madman, Todd."

"Naw, it wasn't me," he said looking over at Bobby. "It was Bobby. I was standing right next to him."

Bobby was a little embarrassed and looked down without responding. Todd was clearly making an effort at some kind of reconciliation, but Bobby didn't know why.

Bobby felt a real camaraderie with all the guys in the trench, even with Todd. They all had something in common now. They all had suffered the same traumatizing experience that bonded them together. Tomorrow and the next day and the day after that would prove whether Todd also felt the oneness with them that Bobby was feeling with him. Maybe Todd was feeling the same way. Maybe that's what his new approach was all about. In the end, though, Bobby didn't really much care. He didn't have the energy or time to care about Todd's problems with him. Although he was feeling drained and exhausted after the fire fight, he was also feeling a lot stronger as a person. Between the V.C. attacking the compound and Todd attacking him, he had somehow hardened his resolve to stand up to it all and fight back. He wasn't going to sit back and just let it all happen to him without some effort to resist it and stand up to it. Bobby was optimistic and he felt good about himself and he even felt good about Todd, in spite of their past.

The Commanding Officer came walking through giving an order to report by field phone to the Sergeant of the Guard, and then told everyone to try to get some sleep. He announced to the men that there would be a company formation in the morning to inform them of what actually had happened this night. Each little group only knew what happened where they were, but no one had the big picture. It would be an interesting formation. He also told them that the Marines were now in the company compound patrolling the grounds, so they could all get some sleep. No one needed to pull guard duty. They were all relieved and exhausted, both physically and emotionally.

Bobby, Joey, and Brad settled in for the night right where they were. Phil and Todd were a few yards away, but the ground between them was too rocky to sleep on, so Todd moved closer to the trio. They spread their bedding and bags out, used their flak jackets as pillows and tried to get comfortable. The weather was cooperating and not raining, although it was warm and humid, even at three in the morning. It was pitch black at the bottom of the trench and they couldn't see a foot in front of them. They felt safe in the darkness from Todd's prying eyes. Bobby lay between Joey and Brad and they both rolled towards him. Brad put his arms around him, but Joey just positioned himself very closely.

Bobby turned his face to Joey and said in a whisper, "I still love you."

Joey leaned forward and kissed him on the forehead. Bobby stretched upwards and just lightly touched his lips to Joey's. Joey didn't pull back, but he didn't press forward, either.

"Thanks," Bobby said and rolled over into Brad's arms.

"G'night, guys," said Todd in the darkness. The other three looked at each other and started laughing.

"What's so fucking funny?" Todd asked.

"Nothing. G'night, Todd," said Joey and everyone drifted off to sleep.

The entire company was in formation in the middle of the company compound at 07:00am. The company commander was standing in front of them and with a microphone began his address.

*"Men, we've had a stressful week and a very stressful night. For many of you it was the first time in battle and I'm sure, although you were scared, you pulled it together and you did your duty. I have to tell you now, though, we've lost our field station here. While many of you were fighting off the enemy, the swing shift was forced to destroy all of the equipment and burn all of the documents in ops. There's nothing left. As you know, in the case of being overrun by the enemy, we are ordered to use white phosphorous grenades on all electronic equipment and burn all top secret and top secret–codeword documents. This we did last night. Many of your hootches were destroyed in the rocket attack and most of our radio towers were destroyed as well. We have no effective reception at this point. We are lucky, though, that we did not lose one single man last night. The official body count by the Marines was 83 dead V.C. And they were not successful in overrunning our company. I congratulate you on your skill, your bravery and your responsiveness to this crisis. We will have to bivouac here for a day or two and then you'll all be given new orders and transferred to new duty stations until your time to rotate back to the States. I want to thank you for a job well done and tell you all that I was proud to be your company commander. Good luck, men."*

When he finished, the C.O. walked away and that's the last time any of the men ever saw him. When the men were dismissed, Bobby and Joey Dee walked towards each other. They stopped and just looked, then gave each other a big hug.

"You know what's going to happen, don't you?" asked Bobby.

"I think so," said Joey. "I can feel it. We'll be sent to different duty stations."

"We can think positively," said Bobby. "Maybe not. Maybe we'll get lucky."

Joey smiled and said, "Yeah, maybe so."

"You know, I was scared last night," added Bobby. "But not nearly as scared as I am right now."

"I'm terrified," said Joey.

Brad and Todd walked up to them and Todd asked, "Can you believe it? After all that, we're all gonna be split up in different companies."

Bobby and Joey looked at him and smiled. Joey said, "It occurred to us, too."

"Hey, what are you two love birds gonna do, if they split you up?" Todd asked with some sincerity.

"I'm straight, Todd, you know that," said Joey.

"I know, sorry, but what are you guys gonna do, if they send you different places?" he asked again.

"We'll just have to learn to write," Bobby said. And they all laughed. Brad stepped forward facing the small group. His eyes made a quick sweep of the area and his facial expression revealed that he had something to say.

"I met Wharton, the company clerk, when I first came in and, after talking a while, I found out we go to the same church. Same church as you, Bobby. I might be able to talk to him about some of these transfer orders. He may not have any influence, but I could ask, if you all think that'd be helpful," offered Brad.

"Far out," said Todd. "If I'm gonna be transferred, I'd like to be with guys I know. If you got any pull with him because of your religion, hey, use it, man."

Bobby had to keep himself from laughing, realizing that Todd didn't have any idea what Brad meant. "Yeah, I'm with Todd. Maybe we can all be reassigned together."

"Bobby, why don't you come with me? We'll go talk to Wharton. See what he can do for us," suggested Brad.

"Ok, let's go," said Bobby with some enthusiasm.

"Come on, Todd, you're looking pretty grimy," said Joey Dee. "Let's go take a hot shower, get cleaned up."

"Hey, yeah, how 'bout that!" exclaimed Todd. "They didn't hit the latrines! We can still take a shower!" Joey and Todd started walking away, but Todd turned around and said, "Oh, Bobby, by the way, I know it's probably too little too late, but I'd like to apologize for calling you a faggot. I don't understand it, but our talk last night was, well, interesting. And I watched you in the firefight, and, man, you were somethin' else! You were right in there with the best of 'em. A fag...oh, sorry man. I mean a gay guy wouldn't or maybe couldn't do that."

"Thanks, Todd. Apology accepted," said Bobby graciously. "But there are no heroes here. We all did it together. You and I did it together, and I'm still queer." Bobby smiled and raised his eyebrows in recognition of his double entendre.

"Well, if you are, you ain't one of those pussies. You did good," Todd said with clear sincerity.

"OK, Todd, I did good. Thank you," Bobby said still smiling, but this time more condescendingly. As he and Brad walked away he commented, "I can't help but think there's some sort of strange order to all of this. Todd apologizing like that."

"I don't know, maybe," said Brad. "Or maybe he's just smart enough to learn."

"Oh, he's smart enough to learn, but to want to—that desire to learn comes from somewhere," said Bobby thinking much more deeply about it than Brad was in the mood for.

"Come on, Bobby, let's find out what's up with those transfers," Brad said.

Bobby and Brad walked over to the makeshift tent that had been set up to replace the company office that had been destroyed in the attack. Jack Wharton, the Specialist 4 company clerk, sat at the desk in the tent filling out paper work. His fatigue uniform was slightly dirty, his hair in disarray and his young face was showing the shadows of a couple days without shaving.

"Hey, Wharton," Brad said in greeting. "Looks like your job's gonna be hell over the next couple days"

Wharton looked up. "Hmm...hey, Brad. It ain't a pretty picture here, that's for sure. I've already received a teletype from MAC-V through the field station down the road in Qui Nhon. They've listed how many guys are needed in the different stations around the country. I'm just supposed to alphabetize and divide up the guys between all these companies on this list," explained Wharton.

"Does that mean that you decide who goes where?" asked Brad.

"No, not exactly," Wharton answered. "The names have to be in alphabetical order, and if they're not, then it's my ass."

"When will the orders be cut?" asked Bobby.

Wharton looked at him, hesitated momentarily, then answered," Today and tomorrow. Most of you guys will have to ship out by tomorrow night at the latest."

"Man, this is happening too fast," said Brad. "How 'bout yourself? Where will you go?"

"I don't have any idea, really, but it will be the last group out, like you, since our names start with a W."

"Yeah, guess so," said Brad somewhat absent-mindedly. He turned to Bobby and said, "Well, then, let's go get ready to ship out. Doesn't look like there's anything more we can do."

Bobby and Brad walked away from the tent towards the destroyed and burnt out hootches. They had to pass the old club on the way. It was still standing but looked rather pathetic and dilapidated. No one had used it since that mortar attack a couple months earlier, when Lien and Joey were hurt. Bobby stopped in front, pulled the damaged door aside and looked in. The bar was still in tact, but the refrigerator and popcorn machine were destroyed and covered in dirt. There was an old mattress in the corner on the floor that had not been there before. Bobby looked at it, looked back at Brad, grabbed his hand and led him inside. "I don't know where the mattress came from, but I'm glad it's here!" Bobby exclaimed. "I want you to fuck me, Brad. I need you to put me out of my misery."

"Shit, Bobby, you make it sound like a mercy killing," complained Brad

"Well it is, isn't it? After everything that's happened, I feel like my old self is fixin' to die. The only way I can start over is with you—this way. I wanted you already last night in the trench," Bobby admitted.

"In the trench?" Brad exclaimed. "I thought that disgusted you."

"Well, it did at first, but after the attack, I was so horny I was willing to do it right in front of Todd!" Bobby exclaimed with a mischievous smile. "But this mattress is about all we got now. So how 'bout it?"

Brad unbuckled his belt, dropped his fatigue pants and stepped out of them. He leaned over, untied his boots and pulled them off. Bobby watched until Brad's boots were off then he, too, started to undress. Brad moved over to the mattress, took his shirt off and laid himself down, erection side up. Bobby stripped naked and joined him. He lowered himself over Brad's body and kissed him passionately. He looked deeply into Brad's eyes, smiled and said, "Cocktails, anyone?"

Brad laughed, pushed him off and forced himself on top of Bobby. Bobby spread his legs and wrapped them around Brad's waist. "Do it, Brad," Bobby commanded. "Please." Brad leaned down, passionately kissed him and penetrated him gently but firmly. Bobby's jaw opened as he felt the heat from both Brad's dick and the friction it caused. They fucked for an hour. Their pent up nineteen-year-old sexual energy and the stress from the battle the night before created in them an intense sexual desire that they both allowed free expression. Afterwards, they lay sweaty and exhausted in each other's arms and dozed off for a few minutes.

After being fully awake again, Bobby smiled at Brad and said, "I didn't really know what it would be like. It's only been a fantasy and, it's true, you really do have to be there."

"Yeah, I guess so," Brad agreed with a smile. "So, you still turned on to it? Sex with men, I mean."

Bobby chuckled and said, "I think so. It took me a few minutes to get used to it and figure out what I was doing, but it works for me, so, yeah. I'll definitely do it again, if that's what you're asking."

Brad slapped him lightly on the butt and said, "We gotta get up. The guys'll be looking for us."

Bobby rolled over, got up, and grabbed his fatigues. Brad did the same and they dressed and walked out of the club together. As they walked back to the center of the company, they noticed that some men were lining up at Wharton's desk under the tent. They saw Todd and Joey Dee standing in line.

"Hey, Joey, what's up?" asked Bobby as they came closer.

"All of us with the last names from A through D are getting our orders. We're shipping out already this evening," explained Joey. He looked at Bobby and the sadness was very clear in his face.

Bobby turned to Brad and barely masking his emotion said, "I'm staying here with Joey, OK?"

Brad nodded and said, "Sure. I'll just take off for a while. See ya later."

Bobby nodded and walked over to stand next to Joey Dee. Todd Churchill was next in line then Bill Daniels and then Joseph Diefenbach. Both Joey and Bobby were fighting to hold back the tears. Todd knew what the situation was between them, and although he didn't completely understand or sympathize, he was beginning to accept the profound closeness and intensity in their friendship. He stepped up to the table, leaned over and signed some papers, then picked up his copies and walked away reading them. He turned to Joey Dee and Bobby and said, "Canto, down in the delta." Joey nodded in acknowledgment. Daniels signed his papers and walked away. Joey stepped forward, looked at the papers to find the name of the new duty station. He signed at the bottom and picked up his copy. He turned to Bobby and said, "MAC-V Headquarters in Saigon."

"At least I know where to write to you," said Bobby. "As soon as I get to where I'm going, I'll write and tell you about it, OK?"

"Fine," said Joey Dee. With tears in his eyes, but not crying, he said, "I have to go, Bobby. I have to get my shit together."

"What time do you have to leave?" Bobby asked.

"They're bringing in a deuce-and-a-half to take us to the airbase. It's supposed to be here any time," said Joey. "Hey, where were you anyway? I tried to find you, but I couldn't find you anywhere."

Bobby smiled, looked down and said, "I went for a cocktail with Brad."

Joey started to laugh and cry and the same time. "Well, con...gratulations!" he said through a small, but tearful sob. "You finally did it, huh?"

"Yeah, I finally did it," Bobby responded looking affectionately at him.

Neither spoke for a brief moment, then Joey said, "I'm gonna miss you so much."

Bobby nodded and said, "Me, too. Be careful, Joey. I want to see you in Ohio when this is done." Joey nodded and said, "You, too."

A truck veered into the compound and came to a stop in a cloud of red dust in front of Bobby and Joey. "I have to run to the trench and get my duffle bag. Wait here for me, OK?"

"I know, Joey. Just go," Bobby said with an emotional smile.

Bobby waited. It felt strange to stand there alone in the middle of the ruins of the company. He looked around and the violence of the night before encompassed the entire space. The men with names beginning with A through D began climbing into the back of the truck. Joey and Todd came running with their combat gear and duffle bags. They threw the duffle bags into the back and climbed up. Bobby walked over to the truck and stood there looking up at them. Wharton came out with a list and began to call off the names. After each name, someone yelled "here". When he got to the end of the list he yelled to the driver, "Airbase! Take off!" And the truck pulled forward. Joey Dee raised his hand in good-bye. Bobby Pinks did the same. Todd saluted Bobby, which surprised him so much he couldn't react. He was left standing in a cloud of dust. When the truck was out of sight, he turned slowly and walked back down the center of the company.

He looked up and saw Brad in the distance standing in the middle of the destruction. Bobby slowly approached him clearly feeling the grief and the loss. Seeing the emotion in his face, Brad put his arm around Bobby's shoulders and walked with him to a nearby bunker where they spent the time waiting for their turn with Wharton. The night was uneventful and the two men comforted each other in the face of the unexpected changes. They talked about Joey Dee and reminisced about the horrors and the wonder of the last five months. Their tongues were tired, their eyelids heavy, and their minds wandered as they tried to stay awake and keep each other company. Sleep eventually won out. They fell asleep next to each other in the bunker.

They woke up the next morning to silence. No alarms, no reveille, no yelling. They emerged from the bunker and saw Wharton's tent surrounded by men waiting for their authorization and new assignments. They each learned that morning where they were being reassigned. Brad Williams was going to Quang Tri up near the DMZ and Bobby Pinks was assigned to Cu Chi between Saigon and the Cambodian border. Bobby was on the second to the last truck for those names beginning with M through P. It pulled out at a little after 01:00pm. It was another unsatisfying good-bye. He sat in the back of the truck and just nodded his head at Brad who was standing where he had stood the day before. The truck pulled out, leaving Brad standing in the same cloud of red dust. Bobby watched him disappear in the distance as they both waved good-bye. When the truck finally hit pavement, the cloud of dust settled and Bobby watched the passing landscape on the way to the airbase. He felt a certain sadness but also relief. It was finally over.

They had all left, each going his separate way. It was September 1968 and the end of Bobby Pinks' first five months in Vietnam. His time in Da Nang with those men had been a life changing experience—the most intense and formative five months of his entire life. He was a different person. The old Bobby Pinks shed his adolescence in Da Nang. That young boy was gone—destroyed by the choices he had made and the circumstances of his life there. The new Bobby Pinks, a gay man, was reborn. The experiences shaped a new set of values and goals, defined who he was to become, and everything that happened to him thereafter. He thought back to the flight from

Oakland and how he had sung "The Fixin' to Die Rag," and then to that first day in Saigon walking into the Ton Son Nhut terminal. He remembered how he felt like he was marching to his death—like walking into Hades. It had actually been a premonition of what he would face in Da Nang. He now realized there were all kinds of deaths and that each one led to some form of renaissance or resurrection. He had taken an amazing journey through the deconstruction of the young child, Bobby Pinks, to the rebirth of a more authentic, mature person.

He finished his tour of duty in Cu Chi, which was relatively uneventful in comparison to Da Nang, and went back to Washington, D.C. until he separated from the military. He never went back to Bismarck. He decided to make a life in Washington. Joey Dee didn't extend his tour of duty in Vietnam as he had planned. He was sent to Bad Aibling, Germany for a year and a half before his separation from the military. He returned to Bowling Green, Ohio, settled there, got married and raised a family. Brad extended his tour in Vietnam another six months and then was re-assigned to the Presidio of San Francisco until he got out. He stayed in San Francisco after that as so many other gay people had done over the years after military service. The three men stayed in contact for a few years after their time together, but eventually their communication stopped as they settled down, readapted to civilian life and lived their lives. They never did see each other again after Da Nang and no one ever heard from Todd again.

In looking back, Bobby realized Da Nang was a perfect experience—a perfect crisis that shaped his soul and forged his character. He never forgot Joey Dee or Brad or Todd, but he never felt compelled ever to seek them out again after their communication had come to a gradual end. Bobby was fully confident in his life and himself. He had been very emotionally dependent on Joey and Brad back then, but that was then. He was Bobby Pinks, a Vietnam veteran, yes, but also a gay man who could now cope in a straight world without loathing himself. He was a part of a new generation of homosexuals, who would stand up for themselves and advocate for their own well-being, equality and authenticity. Bobby had strength and purpose and he was not afraid to fight.

# cherry boy

G.D. Lorentzen

Ben Linden arrived at Ton Son Nhut Airbase outside of Saigon on April 29th, 1969 with a group of colleagues from the Army Security Agency Training Center near Boston. They were linguists, Morse code intercept operators, senders, analysts and cryptographers. The group from Fort Devens, Massachusetts was housed in the St. George Hotel in Cholon, the Chinese district of Saigon. Ben and the other Morse code intercept operators spent four days there processing into the country for their one year tour of duty in Vietnam. They were cherry boys—nugs—Vietnam virgins—new guys—and they looked it in their fresh olive green fatigues, not yet bleached grayish white from the intense tropical sun. They weren't self conscious about it in Saigon—everyone was new in Saigon. But the group was then transported to Long Binh about an hour north. There they met seasoned veterans of the war and it wasn't just because their uniforms showed the wear and tear of the climate, but also because their souls and minds were tired and worn. It was there that Ben began understanding what it meant to be a nug—to be a Vietnam virgin. And, like the others, Ben began feeling self conscious about it.

He wasn't sure what they were doing in Long Binh, unless it was just a holding place until transportation and accommodations could be made at their new duty station. It seemed a waste of time. He was getting anxious to become experienced in the realities of Vietnam. But in Long Binh, they did nothing but eat and sleep. There was nothing else to do. He and the others speculated about the situation, but there was no point in asking anyone. It was the Army. It was Vietnam. Things happened—just because.

After only a couple days in Long Binh the group was divided up and sent to various places around South Vietnam. Ben and a few others flew in a C-130 troop transport from Long Binh to Phu Bai on the northeastern coast of South Vietnam somewhere between Hue and Da Nang. He was trucked from the airbase there to the nearby 8th Radio Research Field Station. When he arrived he was led to an old French colonial stucco building somewhere in the middle of the camp. It was relatively late at night by the time he was assigned a bunk and locker. When he walked into the building, the lights were on and other newly arrived soldiers were making beds and unpacking duffle bags. Ben took his mosquito netting and constructed a mosquito and insect proof shelter around the top bunk. He tucked the netting under the mattress to ensure that no annoying insect could get inside. He was rather tired from the traveling, so he put everything in his locker, closed the combination lock, hoisted himself up to the top bunk and promptly fell asleep.

Sometime in the middle of the night, he was awakened by a loud noise and intense concussion around his head. It was like the concussion one feels when doing a cannonball off of a diving board or platform into the water. He gasped, but couldn't breathe and everything smelled and tasted of dirt and mold. As his senses returned to him from the unconsciousness of sleep, he began hearing voices yelling and swearing in the dark and among the voices he heard the alarming word 'attack.' He rolled to his left to jump off the bunk, but found himself completely entangled in the mosquito netting with which he had so carefully encased his bed. He struggled with the netting until he fell rather unceremoniously to the concrete floor. He then crawled over to his locker where he met his bunkmate, one Sam Garcia from El Paso, Texas, also on his hands and knees trying to get into his locker. They had both locked up their uniforms and gear with a combination lock and it was too dark to see the numbers to open them. Neither of them had a lighter or flash light. They began to realize that a number of other guys in the building were in the same situation.

"So what do you guys think we should do?" Ben asked in a whisper.
Some voice out of the darkness said, "Well, they said there's a trench that surrounds the area, so we might just go out and whatever direction we go, we should find a trench."

"OK," Ben agreed. "Let's try it."

They walked out of the door, all of them in their military issue, olive green underwear and barefoot, and began walking in silence in the darkness. Suddenly, there was a whistling sound, a thud and another concussion accompanied by an explosion of light and fire not too far off in the distance. They all instantly hit the ground and began crawling. They didn't get very far and someone said in the pitch black of the night, "What the hell are we doing? We don't know where the fuck the trench is. I think we should turn around and crawl back."

They all agreed, got up and ran back to the building. By that time the rocket attack had ended, they were all back in bed. As Ben lay there on the top bunk, he realized that a rocket, mortar or bomb of some sort must have landed very near by and the concussion had loosened all the dust and dirt in the rafters. All that dirt had landed on his mosquito netting and his face. That's why he couldn't breathe and why he tasted and smelled dirt and mold. Suddenly, the door swung open and all the lights went on. Some unknown captain was standing in the doorway. He took one look at the few young soldiers in their bunks and began screaming, "What the fuck you idiots doing in bed?! Do you realize there's a rocket attack goin' on outside and you're lyin' in bed like y'all were on some vacation in the tropics!? Git yer asses outa those bunks, get yer gear on and get the fuck outa here! Come on you simple–minded mother fuckers! Move yer asses out to the trenches!"

They all jumped out of those bunks, and with the lights now on, they could open the lockers to get out their gear. Ben was dressed in a matter of seconds and, together with the small group, was running outside following the Captain's index finger to the trenches. Everyone spent the next hour or so out there, then they were told to go back and go to bed.

That was his first night in Phu Bai. May 8th, 1969. The rocket that so impolitely woke him up had hit just across the way in front of the club. So the club was closed temporarily until repairs could be made. Luckily, no one was hurt or killed in the attack. That was how his stay in Phu Bai started and it only got worse. Those rockets came in a few times every week disrupting his sleep and keeping him grouchy and somewhat ill tempered. It also didn't help his mood that the officers felt the base was a show place for the Brass from stateside who came to Vietnam on temporary duty (just to say they'd served in Vietnam, everyone was sure). So, soldiers were constantly harangued to keep their uniforms clean and pressed, boots highly polished and hair closely cut.

To add to the pressures, the work schedule was grueling. Ben worked from May 9th to sometime in mid–August twelve hours a day, seven days a week without a single day off listening to the electronic dots and dashes of Morse code. The weather was hot and muggy and the dirt was like rust red talcum powder. It got into everything, including nostrils, ears, under fingernails, in shaving kits, between the sheets—virtually everywhere. Ben's body reacted and he developed a severe sinus–infection that landed him in the field hospital in Da Nang for two weeks. That was all bad enough, but then monsoon season hit and the rains came and Ben's suffering became exponentially worse.

During that monsoon season of 1969 in Phu Bai, the rains were so heavy the whole area was turned into a giant lake and the roads became gooey, rust-red mud paths. Those who were unlucky enough to find themselves on guard duty experienced the worst of it. That guard duty should fall on Ben's shoulders during the heaviest part of the rains, struck him at the time as just retribution for having just spent two weeks lounging on China Beach in Da Nang with a sinus infection, slurping up antibiotics with Kool-Aid and socializing with the orderlies and nurses. Who knows, he probably got the sinus infection from breathing in all that mold and dirt during that first rocket attack.

When he reached the perimeter that evening for guard duty, he sighed with relief to be assigned to the so–called Super Bunker—an engineering marvel of more than a thousand sand bags, three stories tall, with a crow's nest up top that was actually comfortable to sit in. Cyclone fencing stretched 180 degrees around the front of the bunker and reached higher than the crow's nest. Beyond the fencing lay ten claymore mines strategically placed to create an impenetrable wall of defense.

The bunker housed six soldiers—one in each of the two foxholes to the side, two "off–duty" on the ground level, one on the third level, and one in the crow's nest. They were to rotate positions every three hours. His first rotation was in the right foxhole manning the machine gun. At midnight, it was his turn to ascend to the crow's nest, which on this particular night turned out to be the worst position, because the monsoon rains had increased so dramatically that it wasn't even rain anymore. There were simply torrents of water coming down in the blackness and no poncho or raingear could keep anyone dry. Ben vainly spent his time emptying water out of the nest with his steel pot, only to give up because the water was filling up faster than he could empty it.

He placed his helmet back on his head and sat in the water huddled up to his M-14 rifle under his poncho. It didn't matter anymore that he was sitting in two feet of water. All six men in the bunker were miserable. About an hour into his turn in the crow's nest, Ben heard something out of the ordinary, but it wasn't loud. He looked around but couldn't see anything. Ben called down to the guy in the machine gun nest below, "Hey! Steve?"

"Yeah, what?" Steve called back.

"You hear anything?" Ben asked with concern.

"No, why?" Steve answered slightly unnerved at the question.

"Never mind. It was probably nothin'," Ben said, and he sat back and relaxed. About that time he heard it again, but it seemed very close to his ears. He slowly turned his head to the left and, through the heavy rain, looked into the face of the biggest, ugliest rat he had ever seen in his life. He let out a scream they must have heard in San Francisco! The field phone went flying, his M-14 slid down the side of the bunker, and the phones started ringing up and down the line of bunkers strategically located along the fenced perimeter. His buddies below were in a panic, scrambling up top to see what the matter was. One of them met the rat on his way up and he let out his own prissy, piercing scream. The rat disappeared into the night.

"Holy shit! Did you see that rat?" Steve yelled.

"I did!" Ben exclaimed with disbelief. "And it scared the shit out of me! We'll need to call in, because I know everyone up and down the line heard us screaming . They're gonna think we got our throats slit by V.C. sappers or somethin.'"

Steve found the field phone, called into CQ and told them everything was all right...just a rat...and they sheepishly went back to their positions, more than a little embarrassed by their reaction to the incursion. Ben managed to relocate his M-14, which had fallen from the crow's nest halfway down the right side of the bunker.

About two in the morning, drenched to the bone sitting in a tub of monsoon rainwater, Ben felt suddenly dizzy—like he had vertigo. He sat up with his senses in a paranoid frenzy and realized that the sound of the rain had changed. It sounded like they were bivouacking next to a river. Just then he was forced to lean backwards by some inexplicable force and he could feel a gentle but distinct motion underneath him. Piercing through the raging sound of water and rain, he heard the guys below yelling, swearing and screaming, 'Get out! Get out! Get the fuck out!' Then Ben heard nothing. He realized he was completely submerged in water and there were sandbags above him, below him, and all around him.

At that moment, although he didn't panic, something gripped him from inside and Ben made a heroic effort to stand up. When he did, he was standing nearly waist deep in a flowing river and through the drenching rain he could see the shadows of the others, but there was no bunker. He struggled through the strong current making it over to the others. The six of them stood there speechless for a couple minutes, then barely audible, almost whispering, someone said in the darkness, "fuuuuck." It was one of those long, low, drawn out, whispered expressions one imagines saying if ever faced with an alien from another world.

Super Bunker had been swept away by a monsoon flood. The cyclone fencing had fallen and was under water and they couldn't locate the foxholes with their mounted machine guns. They couldn't find the field phone to call in and they didn't know what to do at all! So they stood there. It seemed like hours that they stood there. Finally dawn broke and the rain began to subside becoming more normal rain and not streams of water.

The six young men spent the entire day out there up to their thighs in murky, rust-red, swift flowing water, before the water level went down enough for a truck to come pick them up. They didn't speak much to each other the hours they waited— probably because of the shock of the situation. The driver of the deuce-and-a-half who had come to pick them up just shook his head and simply asked, "You guys, all right?" Ben just nodded and climbed in. None of soldiers talked at all on the road back to the base. Ben didn't really talk much about the situation with anyone, other than to say with amazement, when asked, "Yup, Super Bunker floated away." The only response anyone ever gave was that simple little expression, "fuuuuck," all drawn out and barely audible.

The flood and the demise of Super Bunker were the last straw for Ben, personally. The sleep deprivation from spending so much time at night in the trenches, the showplace nature of the base, the work schedule, and the weather all made it impossible for him to stay there. He walked into personnel a couple days after the flood and requested a transfer away from the largest field station in the world to a small company somewhere out in the field. Everyone told him, 'No one gets out of Phu Bai.' Or they tried to appeal to his fear by saying, "It's dangerous in the field. You could be overrun." But Ben submitted the paper work anyway, and within two weeks it was approved. In mid–September he was transferred to the 330th Radio Research Company outside of Pleiku in the Central Highlands and he could happily say he never saw Phu Bai again.

Ben was only eighteen years old when he arrived in Vietnam in the spring of '69. He was a typical soldier of the Vietnam era: from a poor family in the Midwest and a high school graduate looking for a way to pay for college. A quiet teenager, young Ben Linden usually just smiled and spoke only when spoken to. He had joined the Army Security Agency at seventeen and completed basic training the week of his eighteenth birthday. He had had his nineteenth birthday at Phu Bai shortly before the demise Super Bunker. Shy and sexually inexperienced, he felt himself to be less of a man than most of his peers in the army. He even suspected that he might be gay. He desperately wanted to lose his sexual virginity, too, now that he was no longer a Vietnam virgin. Yet Phu Bai hadn't afforded him much opportunity to remedy his situation. Pleiku was a different story.

Since in his new unit they were working four days on duty with two days off, they had quite a bit of time on their hands, a situation very different from Phu Bai. Hanging out with new friends, Ben heard discussions about the availability of women in Pleiku. So, on his first day off, he got together with three other guys and they went into Pleiku City, which really wasn't much of a city at all. Pleiku lay on a small relatively treeless plain in the middle of the Central Highlands. It had a small downtown area that had a few restaurants and bars, a tailor or two, and a couple whore houses. Ben had resolved to himself that he was going to put an end to his status as a virgin, if they could find a whorehouse somewhere. The other guys weren't necessarily aware of his motivation for going into town, but the general consensus was that they were going to find a 'house' for some sexy fun. They did find a place that was comfortable, clean and nicely decorated, but Ben wasn't particularly relaxed or focused on his environment, so it didn't matter much to him at the time. The four young men filed into the reception room and there the Madame of the house greeted them with her middle–aged smile filled with fashionable black teeth showing the years of chewing betel nuts. "I am Mama–san," she said. "Fifteen MPC and you have good time! Come! I show you de girls."

As the Mama–san paraded the young women in front of them, one caught Ben's eye and the Mama–san, being the professional that she was, noticed it immediately. She grabbed his hand, pulled him to his feet and said, "You cherry boy. I know. Dis girl do you good time. No problem. No sick. You like dis girl. I can see." She hand–signaled the girl to follow them. Smiling and pulling him along, she took him down a hallway to the right of the reception room. He kept turning his head to look at the girl following them. They finally reached a door and he suddenly had a mild anxiety attack.

He resisted her tugging momentarily, but soon gave in and followed her through the door. She talked to the girl in Vietnamese and gave her a key. The young woman looked at him rather shyly and motioned for him to follow her. They went together down another hall and stopped at a bedroom door. She unlocked it and beckoned him to come in. He was really nervous, but determined to go through with it.

He thought she was very beautiful, but he was anxious that he wouldn't be able to do it—that he was too nervous to get it up. But she was very kind and gentle and was able to calm him down enough to sit comfortably on the bed. She had long, beautiful dark brown hair, translucent skin and a terrific, petite body. She took her clothes off slowly and sat naked in the room window, which looked out onto an inner courtyard. Her silhouette against the bright light of day was stunning. She turned to look at him and her eyes said he should take off his clothes. (He hadn't thought about that until then!) He unbuttoned his uniform shirt and undid the buckle on his belt. She stood up and walked over to him. It was then that he noticed just how beautifully proportioned her body really was. He had been focused primarily on her face and eyes, but suddenly her body was the only thing in his field of vision.

"You cherry boy?" she asked grinning accusingly. His voice choked and he couldn't speak, so he just nodded in agreement. She leaned over and kissed him and then he didn't remember much after that. At that moment he was no longer worried about his performance. Biology took over and, to a certain degree, his mind thankfully disconnected. She knew exactly what to do, when and where. Once she had done her job, though, she jumped up, grabbed her clothes and walked out of the room. He was left lying on the bed staring at the old, brown-stained ceiling, wondering what to do next. He accomplished what he had set out to do, but it wasn't particularly fulfilling as an experience. He was a little confused, because he thought it would be more ecstatic or profound. He had that strange little half–thought, half–question, "Is that all there is?" In reality, he got more out of doing it for himself than with the prostitute.

He got dressed and walked back down the hall to the reception room where Mama–san was waiting. She scurried up to him, grabbing his sleeve smiling her big black toothy grin.

"You no more cherry boy, huh, GI? Dat's good for you!" That rather embarrassed him and to avoid any further extolling of his lost virginity, he took out his wallet, handed her fifteen MPC, smiled, nodded his head and walked to the door. Mama-san started to laugh and said, "You go now, GI, but you come back, OK? Bring friend, OK, GI?"

He just nodded and walked out of the door. He walked into the sun–drenched brightness and tropical heat of the day, looked around and sat on the steps waiting for the others to come out. He inhaled deeply and thought about what he had just done. Panic suddenly gripped him, when he realized he hadn't used a condom!  He had learned in basic training that one should always urinate after sex and that would help reduce the risk of venereal disease. He didn't really know if that was an old wives' tale or if there was any truth in it. Rather than risk it, he jumped up, ran back into the house, found the bathroom and took a leak, then grabbed the soap and scrubbed the Little Man until he thought he was chafing the skin. His heart was pounding and his hands were shaking. Cleaning up eased his mind a little, but he was still slightly nervous that he would come down with the some rumored, incurable syphilis or gonorrhea or even an annoying case of the crabs. He heard the voices of his friends talking to the Mama–san, so he went back into the reception room. They paid and they all left the house together.

The others were graphically describing their respective experiences as they walked through the streets of Pleiku, but Ben couldn't figure out how to explain his.

"Hey, Ben! You're awfully quiet!" remarked Sam, the shortest of the trio. "Pretty amazing women in there, man! It's a little different than with the girls at home."

The others gushed in agreement and their chatter covered Ben's confusion. Ben just nodded and smiled at everything they said. He would've had to reveal that he had been a virgin until that moment. Not an option. He would've had to say that it wasn't all that great. Also not an option. He figured that he should just smile and nod, and not give them any more information than they needed.

In the end, he didn't come down with anything unseemly and he felt an adolescent inflation of his male ego. He could at least say he wasn't a virgin. He felt like he was a primordial man and no longer a boy. He had that still unripe, self–and penis–centered attitude that made these young soldiers feel like Tarzan. He had made the long awaited passage from neuter child to Male, and in the transition, he became stupid from delusions of grandeur and invulnerability—even if the sexual experience with the woman really had not turned him on that much. That fact could be held from public consumption until he could figure out what really would turn him on. In spite of his confusion and disappointment over the experience, he also felt an archetypal fellowship in a male fraternity of sex and war that only a nineteen–year–old soldier can feel. By the time of his twentieth birthday, young Ben Linden was back in the States completing his hitch in the Army. He was newly experienced in both love and war and other, less experienced young men looked up to him. In the reflection in their eyes, Ben saw himself as a man and he nodded to himself with contentment that he was no longer a cherry boy.

# the raunch

G.D. Lorentzen

Payday in Vietnam. It was the last payday of 1969—December 31st, New Year's Eve, on the hill above Lake Bien Ho outside of Pleiku, Vietnam in the Central Highlands. The locals actually knew what we did there at the 370th Signal Research Company. They called it 'Listening Hill.' And it was supposed to be top secret. Well, that's the way things went during the Vietnam War. It was rife with irony and cynicism from the highest levels in Washington D.C. to the private out in the jungle. We weren't immune from it either in our unit. Knowing that the locals knew what we did made us all feel a little odd, perhaps a little vulnerable. We all had top secret clearances and if the VC or the NVA knew what we did, it was conceivable they'd maybe try to stop us from doing it. Such pressures led to rather creative, if not inappropriate, behaviors and expressions. One of those creative, perhaps inappropriate outlets, was called a 'raunch', and it had to do with payday.

I don't remember how it started, or who started it, but for a few months in early 1970, beginning with the last pay check of 1969, we held three day long parties, someone dubbed 'raunches.' We had experienced through the fall of 1969 a dearth of good beer, alcohol and food. The mess hall was terrifying. We couldn't identify the meat, if it was meat. Ice cream was an odd thing. If we let it sit and melt, it wouldn't. It simply puddled a little and a spongy, fibrous substance would be left behind. The only beer we had in our pathetic little 'club', which was nothing but a one-room shack, was Grainbelt in cans. Often we'd open the cases and the cans would be covered in a pale green mold that we'd have to wipe off before we could pop the top. Then the taste was so god awful, I seldom finished one. The only soda pop we had was Fanta Orange and Rooty Tooty Rootbeer. For some reason we could seldom get any cola of any kind. So, that was the situation that led to a creative, albeit questionable solution to the problem.

I don't know who it was anymore, but someone was collecting money, greenbacks only, no Military Payment Certificates, to get supplies for a company party. I began hearing rumors that someone had taken a jeep with a trailer and gone to Kontum to see if they couldn't score some red meat. That was all I heard at first. But on January 2nd, the jeep returned and the trailer was filled with Ba Muoi Ba beer (a Vietnamese brew that was actually pretty good), steaks (water buffalo?), and sandbags of Cambodian Red marijuana. Well, as one can imagine, that turn of events generated quite a bit of excitement in the company. Word spread quickly and that evening grills and a large bar were set up, everything was laid out and we had ourselves a party.

I was working swings at that time, but we had a great work schedule at that point, four days on, two days off. And I was lucky enough to have my two day break beginning on the evening of this first raunch. I was in my cubicle in the long wooden barracks reading when my friend, Dave Blair, originally from Philadelphia, pulled back my blue gingham curtain covering the doorway of the cubicle.

"Hey, you goin' t' the party?" asked Dave with a broad toothy grin.

"I don't know. You?" I asked looking up from my book.

"Think so. Git yer boots on and let's go. I'm hungry. They got steaks on the grill," he said licking his lips.

"Ok. I could use some real meat," I responded sitting up and setting my feet next to my boots on the floor. I slipped into them, tied them and stood up.

"I heard there was good beer, too," I added. "Do you know if they really have some?"

"Naw, I don' know," he answered with disinterest. "But I can't imagine what kind it'd be, if they bought it in Kontum."

"Yeah, you're right," I agreed. "Maybe it's Ba Muoi Ba."

"Hell, even that Vietnamese swill is ten times better than Grainbelt," Dave said with disgust.

"Anything's better than Grainbelt," I said grabbing my hat and walking towards to the curtain.

"I heard they brought some grass with 'em, too," said Dave with a sly wink. "Should be a fun time."

"At this point just about anything different from what we've had for the last three months would be fun," I said with cynicism.

Dave chuckled. "We're getting a new supply officer in February," he said raising his eyebrows. "Maybe things will improve."

We left the barracks and walked towards the makeshift basketball courts where the party was to take place. A number of guys were already gathering around the grills and the row of tables that made up the makeshift bar. As we walked by, I noticed the jeep trailer was parked just off to the side and a couple guys were bent over it and ripping open burlap sandbags with knives.

"Look!" I exclaimed to Dave and pointed toward the trailer. "That must be the grass you were talking about."

"Far out!" exclaimed Dave. "Let's go look!"

We walked over to the trailer and sure enough the bottom of the trailer was lined with some ten sandbags all filled with a very resinous marijuana brought in from Cambodia. Dave and I looked at each other and smiled greedily.

"How soon is that stuff gonna be ready for consumption?" asked Dave.

"Shit, you can take this sandbag full over to the table there on the basketball court, if you wanna," said one guy holding up the bag for Dave to take. "I don't got any pipes, but there's some papers in the Jeep, if you need 'em."

"I'll get the papers," I said, and walked around to the driver's side of the Jeep. There was a plastic bag full of papers lying on the driver's seat. I picked them up and raised them over my head to show Dave. He looked my way and nodded.

We walked over to the tables on the court, set the sliced-open burlap bag down and laid the plastic bag of papers next to it. Without saying anything, Dave opened the bag of papers, took out three and licking two of them sealed the papers into one large one. He then pinched some of the marijuana between his index finger and thumb and rolled it up in the papers creating one large marijuana cigarette that guys often called a 'Bonson Bomber.' He pulled out a lighter, lit it and took a deep hit, then handed it to me and I did the same. The effects were instantaneous. It was fairly powerful grass. Dave rubbed his hands together as he watched me take a hit.

"The food should taste really good after this shit," exclaimed Dave.

The thought of food suddenly made me realize that I really was hungry. I turned my head to look at the grills and a number of the steaks were looking ready. I handed the bomber to Dave and walked over to the table with the plates, grabbed one and waited for the cook to fork one of the steaks and slap it on my plate. Other guys were already standing in line, so I had to wait a couple minutes, but not long. I picked up a knife, fork and napkin then headed for a place to sit down.

"Hey, Dave!" I yelled. "You gonna eat or what?"

"I'll finish this first," he said smiling and gesturing with the Bonson Bomber still in his hand.

Dave smoked a little more, but handed it off to someone else and stood in line for some food. He joined me then, handed me a bottle of the Ba Muoi Ba beer and we really enjoyed those steaks. If they were water buffalo, we didn't know and we didn't care. It tasted like real meat, that's all that mattered to us at the moment.

Soon just about everyone in the company was at the feast, except for those guys on duty on the Ramp. We worked in the back of six two–and–a–half ton covered trucks backed up to a wooden ramp built between them—thus the name. We listened to and copied encrypted Morse code messages sent by the NVA and the VC. I had the impression that we weren't terribly good at analyzing and interpreting the messages, but we high-speed code takers were damned good at copying it with very few mistakes.

Anyway, the party went off really well that night and I don't remember too much after dinner. I woke up in my bunk the next morning feeling a little hung over but it was nothing serious. I looked over my shoulder and was shocked to see Dave curled up behind me. I jumped out of bed and headed for the latrine wondering why Dave was in my bed. I didn't know if anything had happened, but the thought made me smile. Once I showered and ate a little breakfast, I felt pretty good. It was at breakfast that I found out the party would continue all day and night. There was still plenty of meat, beer and grass, so it was decided we should just party til it was all gone. So that afternoon, many of us were back out there, eating, drinking and smoking.

On the afternoon of the third day, we finally ran out of party supplies and we all went back to our normal existence. Neither Dave nor I ever mentioned 'that night'. There was one event that last evening that shook us up, however. About 10:00pm a barrage of mortars and rockets went off over our heads. Everyone hit the dirt, of course, but after a minute or two we all realized it was outgoing, not incoming. The command called the local artillery unit to find out what was up, but the artillery unit wasn't firing any rounds at all. Those on guard duty that night then began looking through their starlight scopes to see enemy soldiers launching mortars and rockets over our heads from the base of the north side of our hill. They were shooting at the airbase some five kilometers south of us. At that moment, one of those mortars or rockets hit the airbase's ammo dump and there was a rumble and thunder like I'd never heard before. The ground shook and the night sky lit up like it was the Fourth of July. The explosions continued for over an hour. We all stayed in bunkers and trenches until things calmed down.

At the time, we didn't make a connection between the attacks and our company party...our 'raunch.' However, the next month, February 1970, again right after payday, the same guys took our money and came back with meat, marijuana and beer and we had another three–day party. This time, however, this guy named Donny Kuhlhorn from Ohio, asked some questions about the procurement of the party supplies. It seems the three guys who got them were contacting rather questionable characters in Kontum, giving them our money in return for the goods, and not asking a lot of questions. Donny theorized that they could be VC and using our money for munitions. He convinced one of our Second Lieutenants to call the airbase and warn them to go on red alert in case there was another attack.

Sure enough, on February 5th, the same thing happened at the base of the north side of our hill. Then we knew that our money was probably being used to finance the attacks on the airbase. It was quite ingenious of the VC, really, because our artillery couldn't target them as long as they were so close to us. We could've ended up 'collateral damage.'

February went by and payday came at the end of the month as usual. The three guys came buy to collect more money for our third raunch. The phone call to the airbase was made warning them that an attack was imminent—probably within the first week of the month. We partied for two and half days, and on the night of the fourth of March, mortars and rockets began flying again over our heads. This time, however, it didn't last long. I was on duty on the Ramp that night and suddenly, instead of the familiar whistles of the outgoing munitions, there was a different sound—an unfamiliar sound accompanied by an unsettling vibration. My colleagues and I looked at each other, slowly stood up then ran off of the Ramp to take a look. It was the strangest and scariest scene. A line of Cobra gun ships, with the sound of their whirling blades punctuating the silence of the night like a strobe light pierces the dark, flew up over the top of us. They hung so low in the night sky, it seemed we could almost reach up and touch them. Once they were in position over the Ramp, they let loose with a barrage of rockets aimed at the VC at the base of the hill. In unison, they reared up slightly and the rockets exploded from their bays attached along side the helicopters. The sound was deafening and terrifying. The attack continued for about twenty minutes and then the helicopters simply flew away. We were left standing in front of the Ramp in a most uncomfortable silence. After a few minutes we walked back onto the Ramp and went back to work. We speculated as to the well–being of our VC friends at the base of the hill. The consensus was they were all dead.

We never had another raunch after that and the VC never set up their mortars and rockets again at the base of our hill. The events that night reminded us that we were really in a war zone. It wasn't a game. Although we still found ways to have fun and party every now and then, we were never again so organized and intense about it. There was a strange quietude and seriousness that came over the company and no one ever again mentioned those three–day long parties that we called raunches.

# house of the rising sun

G.D. Lorentzen

Going to Washington, DC for the purpose of visiting the Vietnam Memorial was difficult for me. I wanted to do it, but I was also forcing myself to go. I really didn't want to be reminded of the war or of myself as a boy soldier—I was only eighteen then. I've come such a long way since then and so much of that time has slipped into distant memory. Only now and then do images and little memories of my time in Vietnam come back to me. The Wall, our Vietnam Memorial, has fixed those memories in black granite and I had been conflicted about seeing it since it was built. As I walked around the grassy knoll onto the pathway in front of the Wall, my anxiety intensified. I saw the black, angular monolith stretched out in front of me. I didn't know what to expect or how I'd react. I stopped for a moment to take it all in and looked at the brochure that I was given to help locate the names. I followed its instructions and walked along the panels of shiny blackness until I found 1969. I looked for August, then with my right index finger scrolled down the list of names until I found his. Specialist 4 Charles Lawrence, August 27, 1969.

I ran my fingers across the engraved granite as if I were reading his name in Braille. I took out the slip of paper and pencil that I had been given at the information booth, placed it over his name and made a rubbing of it. As I did, images of those youthful days came back to me. I thought back to the day I joined the Army and how I knew from the beginning that it would be a life-changing experience. What I didn't know and didn't think about then was the unexpected importance certain people and events in the Army would have in my life. Standing at the Wall, gazing at his name, I began to remember and feel again what it was like to be with Chuck. I would have given anything to be with him again—to feel him, smell him, and hear his voice. I smiled to myself as I remembered him, who I was back then, and how we met. Touching the Wall made the memories seem to come alive and it seemed like yesterday...

I woke up early without the alarm clock, although I had set it the night before to make sure I wouldn't oversleep. It was Friday, June 28, 1968, 05:00am and my life was about to change. I had graduated from high school on June 6th and now twenty-two days later everything in my life would be different. I was joining the Army. As I lay in bed thinking about the coming day, I also reflected on myself and my childhood.

For all of my childhood successes and development, there was something unsettled underneath the accomplishments. My high school years had been good in an extraverted sense, but I still had not come to terms with myself nor had I developed a healthy sense of identity or self-concept. I felt weak and ineffectual in a dysfunctional family with an abusive, alcoholic father and a loving, but very intellectually limited mother. I was tired of being the sissy who had repressed his masculinity and surrounded himself with female friends, but who had very few male friends. I wanted to feel, look and be masculine. I had long ago lost the connection to my male self and I missed it and wanted to feel it again. Missing myself like that made me long for some kind of bond with other males. I was so desperate for it, in fact, that I had turned down a college scholarship and joined the military. I felt this existential need to be surrounded by males and rediscover the masculine part of me that I had begun to reject as a young child. I wanted to bring back the masculinity that I had so thoroughly isolated and locked away in my consciousness. The military seemed an honorable path and the perfect male environment to do that. I also wanted to prove to myself that I could succeed in the male world. I had done so well in artistic and academic worlds, but the hyper-masculine world of the military would be a greater challenge. This was my most important goal, yet I couldn't consciously articulate it and had no one to talk to about it, not even my parents.

Mom and Dad were rather invisible to me. They were there, but we had long ago lost any emotional connection to each other. They drove me from home in Tacoma to Seattle that morning, but we didn't talk at all about my leaving. They showed no emotion about the whole situation, but to me it wouldn't have mattered if they had. My mother initially objected to me joining the military, but Dad said let it be. I knew instinctively what I had to do and I was following some inner, guiding force. That inner force had more authority and power over me than Mom and Dad ever did. I had always paid more attention to it than anything my parents ever said. There was nothing that was going to keep me from this experience.

I was still a child at seventeen, I realize now. I suppose I knew I wasn't very mature, but I wanted to be so badly. Joining the military was a risky and, given the Vietnam War was raging, potentially dangerous approach to becoming an adult male. But I knew it was my destiny. I had had dreams of going to Vietnam for a couple years, but joining the Army Security Agency had also given me options that could have led to other duty stations, or, if, indeed, Vietnam then at least not in the infantry. I wasn't male enough or mature enough, I believed, to be an infantry soldier. I had often compared myself to other boys at school who were physically and emotionally more mature than I. I always came up less in my estimation. I also knew that I was deeply drawn to those boys, but also frightened of and withdrawn from them. The military would be my bridge back to my own kind—back to my male self. That was my plan anyway. But I had no idea how it would all work out.

Mom and Dad dropped me off at the front gate of the Armed Forces Entrance and Examination Station on Alaskan Way down on the waterfront in Seattle. Dad shook my hand and Mom gave me a quick, awkward hug. It made me uncomfortable, so I pulled back as soon as I thought it wouldn't offend her. I picked up my travel bag and waved good-bye. There were no other words exchanged between us. I walked through the gate and disappeared from view through the large, heavy doors.

After a couple hours of military bureaucracy, I was given the oath, put on a bus to Sea-Tac airport and sent to Fort Ord, California for basic training. Basic was difficult and emotionally draining, but I found I had the will and the stamina to do well enough. Although I didn't do exceptionally well in hand-to-hand combat or rifle marksmanship (I barely passed both), I finished in the top three out of seventy-three men in the unit. I did extremely well in first-aid, the mile run, but outdid everyone in the obstacle course and the bayonet drill. The obstacle course was fun for me because I was light on my feet, coordinated and had no fear of heights that would stop me from climbing across suspended logs and other training exercises. The bayonet drill surprised me. It was a fluke in my mind that I did so well, but the drills, with their choreographed movements and prescribed body positions, reminded me of a dance or Tai Chi. Another area in which I did surprisingly well was pugil stick fighting. Opponents were drawn by lottery and I drew someone who apparently was more frightened of this process than I. I soundly defeated him and received a top score. It was a moment of crowning success for me. I had held my own with all these macho guys and, to be honest, I was really surprised. It changed the way I looked at and thought of myself. I could feel my lost masculinity reasserting itself.

After graduation from basic training, I received my first promotion from grade E-1 to E-2. I was recognized and rewarded for performing well, although others received promotions for their leadership skills. As the unit was dismissed for the last time, I felt a twinge of sadness that all this was over. I had grown to appreciate the guys in my unit and I felt a camaraderie with them. I liked them and it was clear they liked me. It was a feeling I had never experienced before. I wondered if I would ever see any of them again. Most of the guys were going on to infantry school and I knew that they would be sent to Vietnam as grunts. I was assigned initially to the Defense Language Institute just down the highway in Monterey. I thought at first I would be studying Russian, but because I already had four years of Russian, I took the D.L.I. proficiency test and passed it. That put me in a holding pattern for a few weeks until the Army could figure out what to do with me.

I was sent home on leave for two weeks, which were uneventful. I didn't see much of my parents, because I preferred to spend time with a couple of friends. Socializing passed the time and took my mind off the Army and my family. The two weeks passed quickly and I had to get back on the plane for California. When I reported for duty at the language school, the officer-in-charge scrutinized my papers, shuffling and reshuffling through them. He furrowed his brow, twitched his nose, raised his eyebrows and pursed his lips until I felt a sense of foreboding.

"Is there anything wrong, sir?" I asked.

"Ah...no...not exactly," he replied distantly. He finally set the papers on the desk, looked up at me and said with enthusiasm, "You're being reassigned to Fort Devens."

"What?" I asked with a clear lack of understanding.

"It seems you were going to be assigned to the Vietnamese language school, but the next cycle doesn't begin for another month. So it looks like they want to give you the Russian M.O.S. (military occupation specialty) and cross-train you in another field," he explained.

"So what does all this mean for me now? Where do I go?" I asked with a little desperation.

The officer handed me a packet of papers that included reassignment orders and travel orders to Boston.

"You have a flight out of San Francisco tomorrow at fourteen hundred hours," he said matter-of-factly. "As for what you do until then, I'll assign you a bunk in the holding company, request some bedding and meal tickets for today and tomorrow and then right after lunch tomorrow come back here and we'll get you on a shuttle to the airport."

The officer filled out some forms, checked a roster, wrote down some numbers and handed me a card with the necessary information to get into the holding company.

"The mess hall is across the quad here, the second building on the left. Dinner is served from seventeen hundred to nineteen hundred hours. The Enlisted Men's Club is open until midnight and the movie theater opens at nineteen hundred. Don't leave the base without a pass and you can't get a pass, so don't leave the base." His voice began to drone the information, then he continued with more rules and regulations. I stood at ease and listened without hearing. I had heard it all before and I knew the routine.

The holding company was located three buildings beyond the mess hall, so I hauled my duffle bag across the quad and through the row of World War II era barracks until I found the right one. I walked up the three short wooden steps and entered the building, which wasn't as modern and clean as my previous barracks in basic training. No one was at the receptionist desk, so I stood quietly looking around at the pictures and miscellany on the walls until someone appeared. I knew it would do no good to explore, because they would just jump all over me anyway, if I were some place I wasn't supposed to be.

Finally, a rather robust staff sergeant, wearing Army issue glasses, probably in his thirties, came out of the back room and with a slightly surprised expression asked, "What can I do you for, soldier?"

"I'm just checking in for the night," I replied directly. I just arrived, but there was some kind of mix up and now I'm being reassigned back East. The flight out is tomorrow at two."

"Y' got yer authorization?" he asked routinely.

I handed him the card the officer had given me. The sergeant stamped it and filed it away in a card file. He reached up to a large board with hooks and keys, took one down and handed it to me saying, "All I got's an extra bunk in a two-man room upstairs. Number 22. Yer sharin' the room with a hold-over. Yer lucky y' got some travel orders. This poor guy's been here two weeks already and ain't seen nothin' yet."

"Thanks," I said taking the key. "What about the bedding?"

"I'll give supply a call. Someone'll bring it over in the next half hour or so," he said helpfully.

"Thanks again," I said as I moved toward the stairs.

"Enjoy yer stay," the sergeant called out. "What we got ain't exactly the Ritz if yer expectin' comfort, but the bunks ain't too bad."

I stopped at the bottom of the stairs, turned my head to listen to the sergeant and replied, "Oh, I don't expect much. I may be new, but I've learned you never get what you expect, so I simply don't expect anything."

"Y' sound like a smart kid," said the sergeant with a smile. "You should get along well in this man's Army!"

I marched up the stairs to the second floor, followed the hallway until I found 22. I hesitated a moment because I wasn't sure if I should knock or simply open the door with the key. I decided to knock. I knocked lightly but rapidly three times, stepped back and waited for a response. I heard someone moving around inside and then the greeting, "Come on in! Door's open!"

I turned the doorknob and opened the door into a room about twenty feet square. I absorbed the details of the room in a matter of seconds. One side of the room had a neatly made bed, posters of Janis Joplin, Jim Morrison and the Monterey Music Festival 1967 on the wall, a small night stand with drawers and a wall-locker for clothes. There was a throw rug with an American Indian design on the floor in front of the bed. The other side of the room held an empty Army bunk and the walls were bare.

A young man about nineteen or twenty was sitting cross-legged on the nicely made bed reading a Mad Magazine. Dressed in olive drab fatigue pants, Army socks and a t-shirt, he looked to be the typical young soldier. His dog tags were hanging over his chest intertwined with multiple strings of colorful hippie beads. He looked up with the realization that he wasn't going to be alone anymore. His brown eyes beneath slightly heavier than normal eyebrows showed a momentary disappointment.

"Sorry to barge in like this, but I've been assigned here for the night," I said, paused briefly, then quickly tried to reassure the guy by saying, "but I'll be leaving tomorrow, so you'll have the place to yourself again."

"Ah, that's alright, " he said when he realized that I was sensitive to his position. "I don't mind, really. It'll be good to have some company for a change."

I liked the guy instantly and found him strangely attractive. He was handsome without being too pretty or too masculine. I walked all the way into the room, set my duffle bag on the bunk and decided to walk over to him and introduce myself. I stuck my hand out and said, "Lonnie Davidson, what's yours?"

"Chuck Lawrence," he replied shaking my hand from his perch on the bed.

"So, the Sarge tells me you've been here awhile waiting for orders or something," I said.

"Yeah, they've been fuckin' around for two weeks trying to figure out what to do with me," he said with disdain. "I don't know what the fuckin' problem is. They assigned me here for German, then found out I'd had some German before. I passed the proficiency test and that's created a problem. I guess they don't want to spend the money to teach me something I already know, so now they have to decide what I'm gonna be doin'."

I chuckled and nodded my head in response. "That's pretty much my situation, too, except it was Russian. "Did you get a chance to request a new school?"

"Fuck no!" Chuck said with a little anger. "It's outa my hands now. I've gotta do what they tell me, like it or not."

"Well, good luck," I said sincerely. "I hope you end up with something you like."

"Yeah, thanks," said Chuck with a milder tone. "Sorry for the little outburst, but the bullshit just doesn't stop around here."

"Yeah, I can imagine," I responded knowing how the military can be.

"What about yourself?" asked Chuck. "Where're you going tomorrow?"

"I'm flying to Boston, " I answered not particularly focused on his question but rather glancing around the room looking at Chuck's sense of style. "I'll be stationed at Fort Devens, but I have no idea what I'll be doing. I don't have a new military occupation specialty yet, either—at least they haven't told me."

Chuck smiled briefly and said, "Well, I don't have an M.O.S. either, so that's a hundred percent more than I know. At least you know where you'll be stationed."

I nodded and flopped on the empty bunk. Just then there was a knock on the door and Chuck yelled to come in the same way he did when I had knocked. A young private came in carrying bedding. He looked around briefly settling his gaze on me and said, "Here...for you. When you check out, just give 'em to the Sarge at the desk."

"Sure, " I said. "Just set them over here," indicating the foot end of the empty bunk. The guy set them down, turned around and walked out without saying anything else.

Chuck got up off the bed and shut the door.

"Talkative bunch around here," said Chuck ironically.

"So it seems," I agreed. I couldn't help but notice Chuck's masculine grace as he moved quickly from the bed to the door and back again. He wasn't muscular, but solid with large upper arms and broader than average shoulders. His waist seemed slightly narrower than I would've expected, with his hips, butt and thighs so well developed. Chuck crawled back onto his bunk, crossed his legs again and seemed to wait for the metallic clinking of his dog tags to stop before he spoke.

"You going to dinner?" he asked.

"Yeah, I'd like to, " I said, sounding more exhausted than I really was. "I haven't eaten since breakfast and I'm getting a bit hungry."

"You know, there's a restaurant in the club where we can get just about anything we want," offered Chuck. "The food's boring, but it's better than the mess hall."

"I've got a little money on me," I replied. "Shall we?"

"Far out!" Chuck exclaimed as he jumped from the bunk, grabbed his shirt and slipped into his boots. "I haven't had anyone to talk to in over a week."

He looked up at me as he tied his boots and said grinning, "Who knows, this could be the start of a beautiful friendship."

I didn't say anything in response. I just smiled, stood up, stretched and walked toward the door. Chuck stood up and with a couple strides caught up with me. He slapped me firmly but lightly on the shoulder and said, "Ready? I'm feeling kinda hungry."

"Sure. I'm ready," I said not quite comfortable with Chuck's friendly attitude and touch. I liked him and his friendliness, but I wasn't quite sure where it was coming from. No one in my life had ever treated me so openly so quickly. I just wasn't sure about it. Or perhaps I wasn't sure about me.

We had a pleasant dinner at the club, but Chuck was right, the food was just so so. We talked about our families, our lives at home and how we ended up in the Army. I really enjoyed his company. We were alike in many ways, but I thought that Chuck was more animated and freely expressive than I. I was surprised to find out that I was, in fact, a couple months older than Chuck. I had thought he was nineteen or twenty, but he was still seventeen. My eighteenth birthday was on August 26th. Chuck wouldn't turn eighteen until December 31st. It gave us an additional bond that somehow had significance to us both. After dinner we went back to the room and talked for hours into the night. Finally, about two in the morning we fell asleep, but we both wished the evening could have continued. We found in each other a brotherhood and a sympathy that neither wanted to let go of. I slipped into sleep wishing I could stay roommates with him. Chuck fell asleep envious that I had an assignment and travel orders. He was beginning to feel useless as a hold-over and it reminded him of his childhood as the youngest of four and the least motivated in the pack of very high-achievers.

I learned a lot about Chuck that first evening together. He was born and raised in upstate New York in the Finger Lakes area southwest of Syracuse. His three older siblings were accomplished and successful. His oldest brother was studying law at Syracuse and his two older sisters were both at the University of Massachusetts, one working on her Masters in Mathematics the other still an undergraduate. Chuck didn't have the grades out of high school to go to college other than a community college. This had disappointed his parents and he was now looking for his own niche in life. He was even considering the military as a career, but if he did, he wanted it to be in Special Forces or at least he wanted to go airborne and jump out of planes. The bottom line for Chuck was getting away from familial and social expectations in order to find himself and his own path in life on his own terms. I felt a kinship with him over these issues. I shared my reasons for joining the Army—those I was aware of anyway—and, although, not the same, they resonated with Chuck in the same way his resonated with me. We found a powerful attraction in each other that led immediately to an emotional attachment.

The next morning, I was awakened by my bladder about eight forty-five. I got up and headed for the latrine. When I returned, Chuck was sitting up in bed looking at his watch.

"We missed breakfast," he said through a yawn.

"Doesn't matter," I said as I climbed back under the covers. "We can catch lunch. I won't notice I'm hungry until then anyway."

Someone began knocking on the door louder than necessary.

"Fuck!" exclaimed Chuck under his breath as he laid back down covering his head with the blanket. "What do they want so damned early?"

"Private Lawrence?" questioned the voice through the door.

"Yeah!" yelled Chuck. "What is it?"

"You got some orders here," called the voice.

I quickly glanced at Chuck. He was lying perfectly still under the covers. He suddenly threw the blanket off, jumped up and swung the door open. The Sarge was standing there holding out the papers in his right hand. Chuck grabbed them and began reading quickly to himself.

The Sarge chuckled out loud and said, "You'd better git yer shit together, Private. Yer shippin' out with this here nug right after lunch. I want this shit off the walls, y'hear? Both of ya, don't forget yer bedding. Why dontcha bring it on down as soon as ya shit, shower and shave. I'll be expectin' ya."

Sarge disappeared from the doorway and Chuck slowly closed the door behind him.

"Who's he calling a new guy?" I asked a little offended. "You're just as much of nug in the Army as I am."

"Yeah, we're both nugs, don't mean nothin'. The only thing that matters is that this new guy has orders!" Chuck said grinning from ear to ear.

"So, you're shipping out with me, today!" I exclaimed somewhat incredulous.

Chuck whooped and jumped onto his bunk with both feet planted squarely in the middle of the unmade bed.

"Yeah, I'm going to Boston!" he exclaimed loudly. "The flight leaves at fourteen hundred hours!"

I sat up and, putting my feet on the linoleum floor, said, "That's my flight! We're on the same flight! That's so far out!"

Chuck began laughing as he jumped up and down on the bunk. "And you know what? I not only know where I'm going, but now I'm ahead of the game, because I know what I'm gonna be doing!"

"Really?" I asked. "What's that?"

"Something called 05H school—wait, wait—let me read it, " Chuck said as he stopped jumping. "High speed Morse intercept. What the fuck's that?"

"Morse?" I asked rhetorically. "Must mean Morse code. Dots and dashes— you know."

"Oh, fuck, I don't care!" said Chuck. "I'm out of here. That's all that's important right now."

Neither of us wanted to wait until we showered to get the bedding down to the Sarge. Chuck jumped off the bed and in a single bound landed right in front of me. He wrapped his arms around me and gave me a bear hug and a quick, loud smack on the cheek. Before I could say or do anything, he let go and said, "Grab the bedding! Let's run it down to the Sarge."

We balled the blankets and sheets together and ran downstairs in our skivvies. By the expression on his face, Sarge wasn't much happy to see us without uniforms on, but he didn't have time to bitch at us. We dropped the bedding on the counter at a dead run and flew back up the stairs as quickly as we had run down. Sarge just rolled his eyes and shook his head from side to side. I heard the phone ring downstairs as we got back to the room, and I heard Sarge's voice as he answered it, but we ran into the room and quickly closed the door.

"Staff Sergeant Wilson, Company C. Yes, sir...yes, sir...right away, sir...Private Lonnie Davidson, yes, sir...oh nine-thirty, yes, sir...will do, sir...thank you, sir...I'll tell him immediately...yes, sir...g'bye."

"I'll be damned," said Sarge to himself. "Those boys are goin' to the same school!"

Sergeant Wilson climbed the stairs, walked down the hall and was about to knock on our door again, when the door burst open nearly hitting him in the face. His reflex was quick and he pulled back just in time.

Chuck looked startled and said, "Oh, Sarge, sorry...hope the door didn't hit you!"

I had to stop very suddenly and nearly ran into the back of Chuck. Sarge looked over Chuck's shoulder to me and said, "you got your school orders just come down. You gotta go to Personnel at Headquarters and pick 'em up at oh nine thirty. Don't be late. There's a bit of a surprise waitin' for ya."

"What kind of surprise, Sarge?" I asked a little excitedly.

"You'll find out. It ain't for me to say," he replied and walked away down the hall. He called out without looking back, "Lads, don't forgit your keys when you check out. I need 'em."

I looked at my watch. Nine-oh-five. "Oh, shit! I've gotta hurry!" And both of us ran down the hall to the showers. We managed a quick shower, chatting with excitement about the prospects of the day. Once out of the shower and in front of the sinks, we stopped talking to concentrate on shaving, although we only needed quickly to run the razor over our adolescent beards. As we were standing next to each other leaning over the sinks, I noticed that Chuck glanced now and then out of the corner of his eye at me. Finally, he asked, "So, you got a girlfriend at home?"

"Naw. Not really," I answered. "I dated a bit in high school, but not seriously.

There was one girl I went out with but I wasn't in love with her. Being in the Army now, I doubt we'll ever get together again. How 'bout yourself?"

"Same here. I was going with this girl in my senior year, but I wasn't in love with her either. We broke it off when I left," he explained.

"I'm not much worried about it," I continued. "I just turned eighteen and I'm not ready for all that yet."

"You a virgin then?" Chuck asked a little too directly.

"Ah, that's kinda personal don't you think?" I asked a little too defensively.

"Sorry, man," Chuck said. "It's no big deal, y'know. I've never had sex with anyone, either. Kissed a little, but that's it."

I was feeling a little embarrassed talking about sex, but I found it engaging that Chuck would just come out and say he was a virgin. "I don't have any experience, either," I admitted.

Chuck smiled weakly, and as he finished shaving, rinsed his razor and dried his face he said, "I didn't think so."

I stopped, looked over at him and asked, "What, it shows?"

"Forget it. It don't mean nothin'," Chuck said walking towards the door. "It doesn't show."

I was feeling a little guilty for being so closed when he was so open with me. I finished quickly at the sink and said, "Wait up. I'm done here, too."

Chuck stopped and waited. When I got next to him he reached out and put his hand on my upper arm just below my shoulder. "I'm sorry, Lonnie, I didn't mean to be nosey. I like you and I want to be friends...I...ah...I was just trying to be open and honest."

"I know. It's OK. Really." I said letting his hand rest on my arm. I couldn't look directly at him though, so I focused on his mouth. "I'm just on the bashful side and I know there's no need to be, but...we can talk about anything you want. I'm just used to being evasive."

"Ok, then," Chuck said smiling and nodding his head. He glanced at his watch, widened his eyes and exclaimed, "Jeez, we better hurry!" We rushed back to the room, dressed and all but ran to Personnel.

Chuck decided to accompany me to Personnel. I thought it was nice that he wanted to. He sat on a bench outside the office and waited while I picked up my orders. When I walked out of the double doors, I had a huge grin on my face.

"What?" asked Chuck with anticipation.

"Oh, five, eitch," I answered enunciating each syllable slowly and very drawn out.

"You're shittin' me!" Chuck exclaimed. "You mean we're going to be doing the very same thing in the same place?"

"Looks that way," I said with satisfaction.

We walked out of the building and all but danced our way back to the holding company barracks. The ocean breeze was cool, but not cold and the air was very clear. Autumn was just around the corner and you could feel it. I took a deep breath and looked all around and said to Chuck, "It's a good day." He just looked at me and smiled.

Back at the barracks, Chuck packed his things into his duffle bag after carefully folding his shirts, t-shirts, underwear and fatigues. We had to dress in our Class A uniforms to fly on military status. We helped each other straighten our ties and button buttons to get it all just right. We had both learned this 'getting it just right' in basic training where recruits were given 'gigs' or demerits for any slight infraction of the dress code. I suddenly removed myself mentally from the scene and realized I was fussing over Chuck. I smiled, my amusement self-contained, as it reminded me of gorillas grooming each other. I felt a growing affection for Chuck and happiness that he would accept my help and offer me the same attention. We stood there facing each other, only momentarily looking into each other's eyes. Looking too long became immediately too intimate and we both had to divert our eyes down to the other's uniform jacket.

When we finished, I commented, "You look smashing in uniform, my friend."

"Maybe, but I'd rather be wearing civvies," Chuck responded. He reached around the back of my collar to smooth it out one last time and said, "I have to admit, you look pretty damn good yourself."

"Come on. Let's go eat lunch," I suggested patting him on the chest. "I'm hungry...by the way, do you have anything to read on the plane? I get pretty bored sitting there for hours."

"So, you think sitting next to me will be boring?" Chuck teased with a glint in his eye.

"Never!" I exclaimed with a smile. "But just in case, I wouldn't mind having something to read."

"OK," Chuck said apparently satisfied with my answer. "There are books and magazines down in the recreation room. We can pick some up and bring 'em with us... no one'll care."

"Sounds good. Let's go!" And we walked off together to the mess hall.

I felt the unison between us as we walked across the quad. I became briefly aware of the fact that we were walking in step, but quickly dismissed it from my thoughts. We turned and glanced at each other simultaneously, completely aware of each other's feelings, but not willing to say anything or make it a mutually stated fact. The emotional relationship that was developing between us was to remain for the moment non-verbal. Our brief glances were enough to communicate the truth. Nothing else was necessary.

Chuck and I flew to Boston together that day, signed into the new company at Fort Devens, Massachusetts and settled into our assigned barracks in a compound affectionately known as "Ditty City." Each barracks had a name and we were assigned to the House of the Rising Sun, named after the popular song by the Animals. We didn't have rooms in the barracks, but rather just cubicles created by the lockers arranged in such a way as to allow some personal space. Chuck and I selected an empty cubicle and moved in. We had to wait for two weeks until our code class began. In the mean time, we were selected for office duties and luckily not for KP or other drudgeries often reserved for young soldiers with time on their hands. Each day brought a closer bond between us and I was quietly thankful that we had been assigned to a company where we could actually share the same space.

After two weeks we were allowed to start our basic code classes. Schooling in Morse code was not particularly interesting for either of us, in spite of our previous anticipation. Our typical day lasted six hours with an hour for lunch. Most of those hours were filled by screaming Morse code at an instructor who demanded ever louder decibels of the chorus. If he felt a particular soldier could yell even louder, but wasn't putting his soul into it, the instructor would place a garbage can over his head and make him scream into it. Or he might also make him stand holding a typewriter with arms outstretched and screaming ditties until the poor soldier collapsed. Chuck and I were both disgusted by the instructional methods, but, of course, were powerless to do anything about it. I vowed to myself that, as soon as I had memorized the alphabet and numbers, I would work to get ahead of the game copying the code as fast as I possibly could. If I could get A.O.G. (ahead of the game), I would have some free time in the afternoon away from the madness.

Both Chuck and I succeeded in becoming AOG and were soon at the top of the class of sixty men. Chuck wasn't as fast as I was, but managed to stay AOG more often than not. When he didn't, that meant, of course, that he had to stay in class for the full six hours a day, five days a week. On the other hand, I soon had almost every afternoon and Friday off, because I was learning to take code so much faster than the others. In fact, I was soon known as a 'super-ditty.' Chuck didn't have nearly as much free time, but enough so that we often were able to spend some private time together in the afternoons. We'd go for long walks in the forested areas of the base, shuffling through the colorful fallen leaves of autumn in New England.

Life in Ditty City was an ambivalent experience. On the one hand, I really enjoyed spending so much time with Chuck—essentially living, working and playing together. On the other hand, military life was becoming annoying and I was having a difficult time maintaining my enthusiasm for spit-waxed floors and spit-polished shoes, buckles and buttons. Chuck, on the other hand, was a military version of Little Lord Fauntleroy. He actually enjoyed the spit and polish, salutes and billeted living. I often felt lucky, in that, without Chuck as a cubicle mate, I wouldn't have been fastidious enough to pass inspections. For Chuck, however, it came naturally, and sometimes, I believed, a little compulsively.

Other guys in the barracks gave Chuck a hard time about his penchant for neat-and-clean. You can always count on compensatory behavior in a group situation like this, just to balance things out. Often they would mess up Chuck's tightly made bunk just to irritate him and make him do it over again. Well, if he loved it so much...

No one every bothered me about anything. Not to my face anyway. I had learned how to hide myself in a group in such a way as to be completely unobtrusive and unremarkable. This particular talent I owed to my family and school situations, where in both cases, being noticed often brought abuse. I was a master of survival strategies like this. In particular, I was very adept at blending in quietly with the character and texture of the group without sacrificing my individuality. I wasn't leadership material at all, but I was always competent at what I undertook, and cooperative, although I never hesitated to complain now and then, when a complaint was warranted. But, in general, I was the perfect team player.

Chuck was also a team player, but he stood out. That had both good and bad consequences. It was often bad, in that the other guys would target him for teasing. Yet, the brass also saw leadership potential in him and consequently promoted him to squad leader. At first, I was devastated, because it meant he had to move into his own squad room and away from me. I didn't know about it at first, because I had gone home for Christmas leave and when I returned I found Chuck's locker empty and his bunk stripped. I was in shock. I quickly ran to my squad leader, Bill Hamlin, and knocked on his door. Luckily, he was in. When he opened the door, I suddenly realized I didn't know quite how to ask about Chuck. I was obviously disturbed, but I didn't want him to see that. So, I just stood there with my mouth half open.

"Davidson, what's up?" Hamlin asked, looking at me with a slight impatience.

"Ah...I just got back from leave," I started somewhat hesitantly, "and, anyway, ah, I noticed Chuck's locker is empty and his bunk is stripped. Just wondering where he went."

"Oh, right," Hamlin said nodding and gesturing towards the stairs. "He's upstairs in the squad room. Forester shipped out and Lawrence was promoted to squad leader, so he's up there now."

"Oh! A squad leader?" I said clearly a little taken aback. "OK, thanks." And I turned around and went to the stairway. I walked upstairs and knocked on the squad room door. I waited nervously, hoping Chuck was there. The door opened and Chuck was standing there in his fatigue pants but no shirt.

"Lonnie!" he exclaimed. "You're back."

"Yeah, um, I just got back," I said a little awkwardly. "So, you're a squad leader! How 'bout that?"

"Yeah, hey, come on in. I don't have much time, but I'm glad to see you...," Chuck said moving to the side to let me in.

"Thanks," I said and walked past him through the door.

"I should've called you or sent you a letter telling you about this," Chuck said apologetically and a little awkwardly.

"Naw, why?" I asked. "I was only gone ten days, so...it's just...a bit of a surprise, that's all. I'll probably have to get a new cubicle mate now, right?"

"No, not unless you want one. I can make sure no one moves into the cubicle, though." Chuck assured me.

"Actually, that'd be great!" I said nodding my head. "Besides, the floors are so spit-polished, I wouldn't want anyone walking on them. I'll keep the newspapers down so the floor won't get smudged."

"That's good. Thanks," said Chuck. "Listen, um, I have to go. There's a squad leader meeting in fifteen minutes and I gotta get dressed."

"Oh, sure. Ok." I said awkwardly moving towards the door. I didn't know how to leave gracefully. I abruptly announced, "I'll see ya later then. Bye." And I walked out the door feeling really awful. Chuck stood in the doorway for a few seconds, but didn't say anything. I stopped briefly, looked at him and waved. He just nodded. Ten days at home and suddenly everything felt different. We weren't cubicle mates anymore and he had to be a squad leader, which meant we weren't going to be able to spend nearly as much time together as we had over the last three months. I missed him already.

Both Chuck and I had finished basic code and were waiting for our advanced code class to begin. Each day I'd go to the bulletin board to check but I never found our names. For some reason, not even the duty rosters had my name on them—that was probably Chuck's doing. I had learned early on that you never volunteer for anything in the Army, so I kept quiet about not having detail and spent the days relaxing, reading and going to the club to listen to music. Chuck was busy with his squad duties and I assumed had no time to get together with me. Although it bothered me, I didn't want to bother him, so I stayed away, hoping he'd come to see me. He didn't. I had no idea that other men would notice the situation.

One evening walking into the mess hall for dinner, an acquaintance sitting at a nearby table caught my attention and asked rather loudly across the room, "Hey, Lonnie! Where's your sister?"

The realization that others noticed Chuck's absence made me blush. I also recognized that the guy's tone of voice was not accusatory, mean or otherwise rude. So, I smiled and said, "She's a squad leader now...I'm sort of a widower, don't you know!"

My self-deprecating sense of humor gave everyone who heard it reason to laugh. The guy decided to keep the joke alive and said, "Well, I don't see you wearing black. What, are you cruising for a new cubicle mate?"

"Naw," I replied. "I'm not up to training a new one."

"I can dig it," he said nodding his head and shoulders at the same time. "Well, tell that sister of yours when you see her that she could at least lower herself a little and come eat with the rest of us peons. After all, we can't let her forget her humble origins!"

"I'll do that," I replied. "Bon appetite."

The guy raised his water glass and said, "To the House of the Rising Sun," and I responded in kind. I thought the guy's little speech was very interesting. I had almost been afraid of being rudely teased about it all, but the guy didn't sound as if he was teasing. The exchange between us was congenial and humorous. I left the mess hall feeling in a better mood than when I went in and resolved to go to the squad room to visit Chuck.

When I arrived at his door, I simply walked in without knocking. I never considered it and I knew Chuck would not be upset by it. Sergeant Todd, the hulky black company duty sergeant, was sitting there with him going over the next day's duty roster. I motioned with my right hand that I'd wait outside until they were finished. Chuck looked at me and nodded his head in agreement, but never said anything.

Sergeant Todd left after about five minutes and Chuck said, "Come in, Lonnie. What's up?"

"Just thought I'd come by and see how you were doing all isolated here in your squad room," I answered.

"Isolated, maybe," said Chuck,"but not alone. Todd's in here ten times a day always wanting something. Sometimes he's a fuckin' nuisance."

"So, uh, how do you like it in here?" I asked.

"What's to like," said Chuck looking directly at me. "I don't have anyone to talk to anymore in the evenings. You haven't come by since you've been back from leave..." Chuck's voice drifted off and he didn't finish his thought.

"Well, I thought you'd be too busy with everything and I didn't want to disturb you," I replied.

Chuck looked slightly dismayed and said, "I haven't seen you for over a week. I thought you might not want to hang around me anymore now that I'm a squad leader...politics...the guys..."

I suddenly felt Chuck's isolation and walked closer to him with body language that wanted to express my condolence. "Chuck, I don't care if you're squad leader. I really thought you were too busy getting into it and doing what you have to do. I didn't want to get in the way and maybe cause you problems," I said with a slightly apologetic tone.

"I missed you," said Chuck quietly without looking at me.

"Really?" I asked surprised. "Then why didn't you come to see me? Why the guilt trip?"

"Ah, it's OK. Don't mean nothin'. I never meant to lay a guilt trip on you. I just thought you'd come around sooner, that's all," Chuck replied apologetically. "I was afraid our friendship was over. If it isn't, let's forget it, OK? It was just a misunderstanding."

"OK. Forgotten," I agreed. "I definitely don't want our friendship to be over."

There was a moment of silence while Chuck put his notebook and papers away. I watched him and I could tell he was feeling uncomfortable, maybe a little awkward.

"So, now what?" I asked.

"Well, what are you doing this evening?" Chuck asked with a certain enthusiasm and a smile as he planted himself in front of me, feet slightly apart, and his hands on his hips.

"Nothing special. Just hangin' out. Why?" I asked.

"You want to go get a beer and listen to some tunes?" invited Chuck.

I thought about it for a moment and I wasn't sure what Chuck's motivation was. I definitely wanted to spend some time with him, so I accepted the invitation. "Sure. I'd like that."

Chuck grabbed his hat and coat, took me by the arm and we headed for the club. We walked in silence through the cold New England air. Neither of us knew what to say. I felt the intense feelings being with Chuck again and it made me uncomfortable. I figured Chuck was probably feeling the same way and didn't push for a conversation. It could wait until we had a few beers and dissolved the inhibitions. We ordered a pitcher, put a few quarters in the jukebox and talked for a couple hours. I felt we had reconnected and wasn't quite so depressed about the changes. After finishing the pitcher, Chuck walked me back to the barracks. Our tongues were looser and our hearts more open, which made the return walk less tense. I huddled up to myself in my fatigue jacket to counter the cold winter air.

"Are you cold?" asked Chuck with concern.

"A little," I answered.

Chuck reached over, put his arm around my shoulders and pulled me closer. "Is that better?" he asked looking directly at me and smiling.

I looked at him and smiled back. "Yeah, that's better," I said. I moved my right arm around his waist and we walked back to the barracks. We separated ourselves as we walked in—instinctive reaction. All the guys were lying around listening to radios and reading as we walked down the center aisle. A few looked up and greeted us as we walked by.

There was a manila envelope lying on my bunk. I picked it up, opened it and pulled out the papers. They were my orders for the advanced school and a new company assignment. I read them and handed the papers to Chuck without saying anything. I had to move to the new company by the next morning. I hadn't been back to my cubicle all day, so I didn't know, and it was already nine o'clock. Moving would be a logistical problem.

"What am I going to do tonight?" I asked myself out loud.

"Lonnie, why don't you just forget it for tonight. Shove your stuff in your duffle bag and we can sort everything else out tomorrow sometime. We'll take just a few things to the new company right now and you can sleep in my room tonight. I don't mind," Chuck offered.

"Your extra bunk doesn't have any bedding on it, though. What am I going to sleep on?" I asked.

"You can sleep with me in my bunk. Don't mean nothin'. There's enough room for two," he said with a smile.

"OK, if you say so," I said. The thought of sleeping next to Chuck suddenly gave me a small anxiety attack, but at the same time, I felt an unexplained excitement. I had to calm myself down. It actually occurred to me that we could have sex. I chastised myself for even thinking the thought and then completely dismissed the idea. I just didn't think it would ever happen. I glanced at Chuck and he was almost staring at me. It made me a little uncomfortable.

"You want to help me with this stuff here?" I asked Chuck.

"Sure," he said. "What do we start with?"

"How about the footlocker?" I suggested. "The uniforms can go later."

We hauled my footlocker across the center grounds over to the new company. Afterwards we headed back to the squad room and got ready for bed. It was nearly eleven o'clock and I would have to be up with Chuck at six. I nervously sat down on the perfectly made bunk, although I hid the nerves enough to act at least somewhat casually. Chuck just as casually began undressing. I was suddenly torn as to whether to watch him or divert my eyes. I decided to get up, turn my back to him and get undressed myself.

"Do you want inside or outside?" Chuck asked as he pulled his pants down revealing white cotton briefs instead of the Army issue boxers.

"Oh, I don't know as I care," I answered unbuttoning my fatigue shirt.

"OK, then, I'll sleep on the inside, that way if it gets crowded you'll be the one to fall off the bed," he said jokingly.

"Sure, make me the fall guy!" I responded. Now we were both down to the cotton briefs. Neither of us liked the olive drab boxers. We always wore 'civvy skivvies' as we called them. "OK, you have to climb in first, if you're sleeping next to the wall."

Chuck pulled back the wool Army blanket and white sheet, slipped between the covers and slid over to the wall as far as he could. I turned out the light, then sat down on the bed, swung my feet up and slipped under the covers. Chuck pulled the sheet and blanket up to our shoulders and said good night. I rolled over facing away from him and said my good night. There was a very awkward silence between us and I couldn't fall asleep. We lay that way for a while until Chuck put his arm around me and cuddled up close behind me. I became very nervous and didn't move.

"This is nice." Chuck commented quietly then paused before continuing. "Isn't it?"

I still didn't respond. I just lay perfectly still staring into the dark. I was terrified. Chuck was quiet for a moment then asked, "Are you OK?"

I didn't know what to say, and it took a moment for my thoughts to form into an answer. "Yeah, I'm OK," I said quietly, almost whispering.

"Lonnie...," Chuck paused. I knew he wanted to say something else but was having a hard time getting it out. "I can't explain this," he continued finally. "But I think about you all the time. I was so scared that you didn't want anything to do with me when you didn't come around after your Christmas leave. Tell me honestly. How do you feel about me?" Chuck asked in a very serious tone.

I rolled over, faced him and innocently asked, "What do you mean?"

"You know what I mean," Chuck responded firmly looking very deeply into my eyes.

"Well, I like you and, yeah, I was worried you wouldn't spend time with me anymore after I came back from leave," I said casually somewhat avoiding the issue Chuck was raising. "I guess, I felt like you didn't want to be around me anymore. But how do I feel about you?" I stopped, not sure how to say what I felt. I was scared to say it, but the words came tumbling out of my mouth anyway. "I love you." I couldn't believe I said that! My whole body tensed as I imagined that he would get up and throw me out of the room. "Oh, sorry, man," I said morosely. "That just came out and I, uh, I, shit, Chuck, I'll just go, if you want me to. I didn't mean to say that."

He smiled very sweetly, though, and asked, "Is that what this is? Love?"

"You're asking me?" I asked in amazement that he had virtually no reaction. Then deciding to be as open and honest as I could, I said with great trepidation, "I'm so scared and confused about us. I really have no idea what I'm feeling. Love is the only word I think describes it. I haven't really wanted to think about it. I don't know, it upsets me and scares me. to think about it You don't seem too upset, though. So you tell me. What are you feeling about us?"

Chuck moved his head closer to mine and gently kissed me. My head was spinning and my heart was pumping, but I kissed him back. His touch was electrifying.

"That's how I feel," he said with affection. Then nearly whispering he continued, "I love you, too. I know, we're not supposed to feel this way about each other. I've never felt this way about another guy. We're soldiers, right? Or is it just that one of us isn't a girl? I don't know, but somewhere inside of me, I'm not afraid of these feelings, just what others will think—and especially what you think. I was scared of you. I wasn't sure how you'd react, if I told you how I felt."

I embraced him and said quietly, "I couldn't say it, either. I wanted to so many times. It was hard keeping it all inside. I don't know, maybe I didn't know for sure what I wanted to say. But now that we've both said it, what are we gonna do? How do we do this here? We can't say anything to anyone, can we?"

"I wouldn't recommend it," said Chuck seriously. "But if we're careful, we can blend in. There are a lot of guys out there who have good friends—you always see them together."

"Yeah, but are they...," I stopped because I didn't know how to name it. "Are they like us?"

Chuck laughed slightly and kissed me. "Maybe, but we'll never know," he said.

"Let's just be together the way we are and with a little discretion we should be OK."

His words comforted me. I kissed him again and the kiss unlocked the passions and feelings we had. We made love to each other that night, as well as we knew how, given our lack of experience. Afterwards, Chuck started giggling to himself. I asked, "What's so funny?"

He looked mischievously at me, then began singing a parody of 'House of the Rising Sun', "There is a house in Ditty City, they call the Rising Sun. It's been the ruin of many a poor boy. Thank God, I know, I'm one..."

I laughed, put my head on his chest and we fell asleep in each other's arms. I really was in love.

The morning began with a start, when Sergeant Todd zealously opened the squad room door at ten to six and filled the room with his overly alert energy. His gaze fell upon our two eighteen year old bodies soundly sleeping with overlapping legs. I woke up first, saw Todd standing there and gently pushed on Chuck's shoulder to wake him up. I nearly panicked realizing my morning hard–on was resting against his leg right in the Sarge's line of vision!

"Hey, Chuck, it's time to wake up," I urged him pushing his shoulder, trying not to sound frightened.

Chuck moved his leg off of me, looked up to see Sergeant Todd, hands on his hips, looking down at us lying there naked on the bunk.

"I can come back later, if I'm interrupting anything," Todd said with a smirk and a suggestive smile.

Chuck sprang out of bed and said, "No, Sarge, you're not interrupting anything. It's not what you're thinking!"

"OK, man, whatever you say. Ain't none o' my business anyway," Todd said glancing at our naked bodies with an expression that made it clear he knew what had gone on. He then turned and walked out of the room shutting the door behind him.

"Oh, shit!" exclaimed Chuck, rubbing his hand over his crew cut head. "I didn't think he'd come in to wake me up."

"You think he'll say anything?" I asked nervously.

"I don't know," said Chuck with a sigh of resignation. "He's cool, but how cool?"

Climbing out of the bed I asked, "We could be in trouble, couldn't we?"

Chuck smiled, leaned forward and kissed me. "I don't care," he stated firmly. "What are they gonna do, send us to Nam? We're goin' there anyway, right?"

"Right," I said sarcastically. " Wait! You sure we're going? How do you know? And what about our top secret clearances?"

"Well, we'll go to Nam with or without a clearance. What difference will it make?" he said trying to make me feel better. "Don't mean nothin'."

"Is that your answer to everything, 'don't mean nothin'?" I asked a little annoyed.

"Well, there's nothing we can do about it now. Todd saw us naked together on the bunk. We'll just have to deal with it," he said with resignation.

"But we were just sleeping when he came in," I said hopefully.

"Yeah, but we both know why, and I'll bet Todd does, too," responded Chuck.

I looked at the clock and said, "God, I gotta go. I'll see you at dinner time."

"OK, maybe," Chuck said without looking at me. "I may have to have dinner with

Todd and the company commander. More planning. It ought to be pretty interesting meeting with Todd." Chuck's eyebrows rose slightly and he gave me a quick, goofy little grin.

"Well, let me know how he reacts and what he says," I responded. "I gotta check in to the new company and start that advanced class today, but I should be back then after I eat tonight."

Chuck opened the locker, pulled out some clean fatigues and started dressing.

"I hope my orders for school come in soon," he said. "I don't want to be around Todd any longer than I have to. Once my advanced class starts, I'll probably have to move companies, too, so I won't be squad leader here anymore. What a relief that'll be!"

"Chuck, none of the other squad leaders had to change companies when they started the advanced class. What makes you think, you will?" I asked looking seriously at him.

"I don't know. I'm just hoping, I guess," he answered.

I got up, sighed with some frustration, and got dressed. After all the good feelings the night before, I was suddenly feeling disappointed again. Once I was dressed and had my boots tied, I hugged Chuck and left him to his squad duties. He kissed me quickly as I walked out the door heading for my new company barracks. I was a nervous wreck thinking about the damage Sergeant Todd could cause us, but we never heard a word about it. Todd never mentioned it again and I often slept with Chuck in his squad room. My cubicle in the new barracks became nothing more than a show place for inspections. I kept all my stuff there, but most nights I slept with Chuck. We learned to make love to each other, exploring and experimenting on each other's body. We had no guidelines, no preconceived ideas about sex, no concept of any standard, typical approach to sexual pleasure. We just did what came naturally and it profoundly transformed us both. I fell more deeply in love with each night in the House of the Rising Sun.

The advanced code school lasted four weeks. Chuck got his assignment the week after I did, so we weren't in the same class, but he did stay in the House of the Rising Sun and wasn't transferred as he hoped he would be. He had no problems with Todd, though. We both did very well in the advanced school, although there was reason to believe that's not what one was supposed to do. Rumor control had it that the super ditties were the first to get allocated to Vietnam. Those with less skill were often assigned to Germany, Turkey or Ethiopia. It didn't pay to do really badly though, because they supposedly sent you to the Aleutian Islands. Even Vietnam was preferable to the frozen rock and wasteland in the Bering Sea. All of that turned out to be simply inaccurate rumor. My whole class was block allocated to Vietnam. So was Chuck's, although I didn't know it at the time. When the instructor read the allocation, my body went a little numb and I began to grieve silently. I had thought of this possibility from the beginning, but in the back of my mind I truly believed I'd go elsewhere. So much for my wishful thinking. Now I had to tell Chuck.

After class, I immediately went to see him. He wasn't back yet and his door was locked. I leaned against the wall and waited for him. I heard his footsteps coming up the stairs about five minutes later. He knew something was up when he saw me standing at his door.

"Hey," he greeted me as he unlocked the door. "What brings you around now?"

I waited until we were inside the room and the door was closed before I said, "We got our assignments today," and then paused before continuing. "We're all going to Vietnam." Chuck reacted with a sudden turn of his head in my direction. I could see that he was visibly shaken, as was I. He put his arms around me and held me for a few moments. I wanted to cry, but my body and mind were still numb and I couldn't. Chuck then revealed what he had already heard a week earlier.

"I probably should have told you, but last week I heard Todd say the next four cycles of the advanced school were being block allocated to Nam. At the time, there were so many rumors going around, that I thought it best not to add to the confusion," he said.

"So, you're going, too, then?" I asked.

"Yeah. I think so," he replied.

"It's alright, Chuck," I said quietly. "I guess I've always known this was inevitable. We're shipping out in two days. I go home first for two weeks, then to Presidio San Francisco for a month for more training. I'll be leaving for Nam on April 28th."

We both sat there on the bed and said nothing more. After a while I lay down and said, "I'm tired, Chuck. I need a nap."

Chuck took an extra blanket and tucked me in saying, "You sleep, hon. Just rest for a while. We'll get used to the idea soon enough." Then he quietly sat on the other bunk, knees up, feet flat on the bed and he leaned back against the wall. I watched the tears run down his cheeks as he wept silently. We could hear soldiers coming up the stairs. Their noisy boots clomping against the floor seemed to sharpen his focus and I could see him shake off the emotion. I looked up and smiled at him. The look in his eyes was tender but filled with worry. He smiled weakly and said softly, "sleep." I knew he loved me and I felt an overwhelming sadness knowing that I was leaving. He sat there on the opposite bunk and just watched me as I fell asleep. I wanted him to be there when I woke up.

I got up early in the morning on the day I had to leave. Chuck was driving me to the airport in Boston to catch a noon plane to Seattle. Everything was fine all morning long. We got done what had to be done; I dressed in my Class A's, checked out of the company, got all packed and crammed my duffle bag into Chuck's car. We were both upbeat and animated on the trip into the city. I was looking forward to flying as I always did and I simply wouldn't think about my final destination—couldn't think about it. Once we arrived at the airport, I checked my bags and still had about fifteen minutes before boarding. The two of us sat quietly in the waiting area watching the people and only now and then glancing at each other.

Chuck finally broke the silence, saying, "I'm going to miss you, y'know. You better write."

He leaned forward in the chair placing his forearms on his thighs and folding his hands together. He didn't really look up at me, but briefly glanced my way. I had been doing fine until that moment. Suddenly, the reality of where I was going and for how long, the fact I was leaving Chuck behind and wasn't sure when we'd see each other again, sent me into emotional oblivion. I put my head in the crook of my arm and sobbed. Chuck sat up and put his hand on my upper back and patted lightly. It didn't help. His touch only intensified my emotions.

"Lonnie, I'll write every day, I promise. I'll call you at home before you go to San Francisco, OK?" he reassured me, but I could hear his voice cracking with emotion.

At that moment the boarding procedure was announced and I had to leave. We stood up together and I wiped my eyes with my uniform sleeve. As Chuck turned towards me, I reached out and embraced him, resting my head on his shoulder. He reached around and hugged me with the full extent of his arms and the tears poured down his cheeks. We stood there together crying, neither wanting to let go.

Chuck whispered in my ear, "I love you...don't ever forget that."

I tightened my grip on him and responded, "I won't. I love you, too." Then I pulled myself away and without looking back walked up to the attendant and presented my boarding pass. I walked down the ramp into the plane in an emotional daze, not fully conscious or aware of anything outside of my grief. Once inside the plane, I found my seat, sat down and leaned against the side of the cabin, placing my wet cheek against the coolness of the window. I never even noticed when the plane took off. I just sat staring into the sky for most of the flight. I knew I might never see Chuck again. It was just a feeling, an intuition, but the wound created by this separation was so deep, that I could feel it touch a core of my being where there was no time or space, where it was all one and I could see the past in the future and the future in the present. And my future was without Chuck.

I wrote to him just about every day from mid–March until I got to Vietnam on April 28th. After that, I was so busy all the time, that I could only manage a letter every few days. Chuck came to Vietnam three weeks later, but was sent to Cu Chi down south. I was way up north near the DMZ. We continued to write and every now and then talk on the phone. The last telephone conversation we had was on my birthday, August 26th, 1969. Chuck had sent me a tape of the song, "House of the Rising Sun," by the Animals. After I listened to it, I went to the MARS station, which was a communication center, to call and thank him.

"Chuck?" I asked when I heard his voice say hello over the phone.

"Yeah? Lonnie? Did you get my present?" he asked.

"Got it. I just wanted to call and say thanks. It was great," I said.

"Well, Happy birthday!"

"Thanks! It was a pretty romantic present," I said trying to be humorous.

"Yeah, OK," he said through a chuckle. "You know, I'm also glad you called. I've been thinking. I can take R and R at the end of November. We can meet in Sydney for the week. You wanna do that?" he asked with a clear expectation I'd say yes.

"Love to do that! It sounds great," I answered. "Maybe we could time it for Thanksgiving. I'll put in for it right away."

"OK, I will, too. I can't wait to see you again. It seems like forever," he said with a tinge of sadness.

"I know, but November is only three months away," I said. "It'll give us something to look forward to here, y'know?"

"Yeah, you're right." Then his voice became very quiet and I could hardly hear him. "I need to be with you, Lonnie. I love you so much. I'm goin' crazy here."

I looked around the office to check out whether anyone was listening to my conversation, but no one was. "I love you, too, Chuck. Let's just save it for Sydney, OK?"

"OK. I gotta go, Lonnie," Chuck said. "I'll call you next week sometime, alright?"

"OK, til then," I said and the line went dead.

I walked back to my hootch thinking and fantasizing about our future together. I imagined we would live together somewhere after the military. It was my 19th birthday and I felt on top of the world. After that day, however, the letters stopped coming. Two weeks went by and I hadn't received any letter from him. I was depressed and worried. I couldn't understand why he had stopped writing, so I called again. The company CQ (charge of quarters) answered the phone.

"328th Radio Research, Lieutenant Miller speaking."

"Lieutenant, I'm trying to get a hold of Charles Lawrence. He's a Spec-4 05H in your company. Can you give him a message for me?" I asked.

"Lawrence? Oh man, I'm sorry, no. He's not here anymore. We got hit pretty hard on the 27th and he and two other guys were killed," the CQ informed me. "Their hootch took a direct hit."

The news took my breath away. I couldn't breathe. My whole body went into shock. My hands trembled. I managed to choke out a thank you and hung up. I walked back to my hootch struggling with my confusion and emotions. He'd been dead nearly two weeks and I hadn't known. I had never felt such pain in my whole life. When I got there, Big Mike, one of seven bunkmates in the hootch, was the only one there. He was a nice guy from Texas, about six foot five and overweight, thus his name. He took one look at me and knew something was terribly wrong. I crawled onto my bunk, curled up into the fetal position and cried so hard my stomach hurt. Big Mike walked towards me, but I shook my head no. He nodded and left the hootch. I cried for hours and every once in a while one of my bunkmates would come in, see me, and leave again. I finally fell asleep from exhaustion and didn't wake up until the next morning in time to go to work.

Guys asked what had happened, and I just explained that a good friend had been killed in Cu Chi. It took me about a week to feel somewhat emotionally stable again, at least enough to interact with my friends and acquaintances in the company. Those who had known Chuck and me at Devens understood why I was so distraught and they were very supportive. It wasn't long before the word was out and I found out there had been a lot of speculation back at Devens about my relationship with Chuck. Most guys had figured it out. As the guys in the 330th found out, some scoffed and talked behind my back; called me queer. I heard it, and although it bothered me, I was able to ignore it, perhaps even forgive it. Over time, though, some guys cared enough to ask me about Chuck and what had happened. Actually, that pleased me. I wanted to talk about him and I've always been grateful that many of the guys let me do that. I often lay on my bunk, reread his letters, listened to the tape of House of the Rising Sun, and lost myself in the memory of his warmth and affection. It took a while, but I was finally able to move on. I went to Sydney for R and R and imagined Chuck was still with me, and I had a good time. I still missed him, but it was OK. Life was still good. Yet I knew that my life would never be the same without him. I knew that I would remember him for a very long time...

The memories and the grief of those youthful days were renewed by the stark, emotional nature of the Wall, and I started to cry like so many other veterans there. I fell to my knees with my head down, one hand on the black granite, the other holding that little piece of paper with his name on it. It's the only thing I have of him other than the few letters and my memories. And though I still grieve, I don't regret. I learned about the goodness of human relationships no matter what form they take. I learned how to love and how to make love. The military itself trained me to be a soldier, but my love for Chuck taught me the courage to take that seemingly impossible first step that broke through the social and cultural conditioning, my fears and inhibitions, and allowed me to make love to him. I suppose you could say that my liberation from those conventions and inhibitions did ruin me as the boy I once was, but it also released the masculine self that I had so long ago rejected and repressed. Through my military experience and relationship with Chuck, that masculine self, so long hidden, had indeed emerged and become a man. I had come back to myself after all. I had found my masculine self, just as I had wanted, but admittedly not quite in the way I had intended. As I walked away from the Wall and back into my life, I realized Chuck Lawrence was still with me, not just as a memory, but as a part of my self—my being.

I never got over Chuck's death. Not really. I still miss him after all these years. I've never forgotten what he looks like, even though I have no picture of him. Every now and then I even get the faint scent of his body, but I don't know where it comes from. He was my first love—my first passion—and I don't know how to forget him.

*There is a house in New Orleans*
*they call the Rising Sun.*
*It's been the ruin of many a poor boy.*
*And God, I know, I'm one...*

# separation

**G.D. Lorentzen**

The year in Washington, D.C. went by too slowly. The more I looked forward to getting out of the military the more slowly the calendar changed months. I found comfort in my friendship with Willie. We had spent the last four years stationed in the same places both stateside and in Vietnam, but it had only been since we were together in D.C. that our friendship became more substantial. We had developed a good relationship and we both recognized that it was our previous experiences and mutual suffering that had created the strong bond between us.

We lived in an apartment together in suburban Northern Virginia, worked and played together just as we had for nearly four years. This time, however, we were alone in our own place, not in a military barracks with seventy other guys. It made the relationship smoother and more natural. Willie, too, felt comfortable enough completely to be himself in my presence. I could tell that for Willie it was like living with family. It was for me, too. I accepted the arrangement, not thinking much about my feelings for Willie or the future. I didn't confront those emotions until it was time to leave the military, and, of course, that meant separating from Willie, too.

Willie and I received our separation papers on the same day, January 21, 1972. We reported to Fort Meade, Maryland to process the paper work and get out. Somehow it was appropriately symbolic for me that we should be released from the Army on the solar ingress into Aquarius. The so-called New Age was dawning, Vietnam was behind us, but not yet behind the Nation, and the future stretched in front of us as sure and as vast as the sky and the Great Plains would in the days that followed.

"Willie, let's go. We're going to be late!" I yelled down the hall where Willie was still grooming in the bathroom.

"Yeah, yeah! I'm done. I'm coming. What time is it?"

I looked at my watch and said, "We have twenty-five minutes."

Willie emerged from the bathroom, freshly shaven, splashed with Brut, a cheap men's cologne, and dressed exactly like me in olive drab fatigues perfectly bloused at the top of highly polished boots. It was our last day in uniform. Obviously, we knew that, but we preferred not to mention it out of some unspoken superstition, that if we had, it would've dashed our dream of getting out.

"Hey, man, grab the paper work and let's go!" Willie said with his mischievously ironic grin, as if I had been the one wasting time. But then the irony in his eyes softened and his grin turned into a smile as wide as Texas and I somehow didn't feel so anxious anymore. We had both been feeling a little anxious about the future, although we were barely aware of it. We drove down Route 50 to Washington and then the Washington-Baltimore Expressway to Fort Meade without conversation, listening instead to the radio. I don't remember any more what I was thinking. Maybe nothing. It was a day of wonder, really. The kind of day or time when words seem superfluous—when wide-eyed anticipation is one's only thought or feeling.

I was twenty-one. Willie was twenty-two. As we stood there in line in the processing center we began remembering out loud some of our experiences in Vietnam. I suddenly felt older than my years. The images of two young, green men in the war seemed suddenly incongruous, unreal or improbable.

The conversation encapsulated our year and half experience. As improbable and unromantic as the experiences had been, they were, in fact, the normal every day experiences of our lives in Vietnam: Mama-sans cleaning, TiTi the shitburner hauling human waste from the latrines, the ear-splitting roar of jet fighters taking off from an airbase, the rumble and thunder of B-52 raids, the psychedelic sounds of choppers crescendoing and decrescendoing in the distance, tense but often uneventful nights on guard duty, and the distinguishable whistles of in-coming and out-going mortars and rockets. These were the essential sights and sounds of Vietnam as we remembered them. And they gave me a small anxiety attack...or maybe an attack of conscience.

I looked at Willie and realized that we didn't belong in this uniform. We didn't believe in this war. We had gone to Vietnam and extended our tour there for our own personal reasons. Willie was the artistic type and I had fantasies of acting, and we both leaned to the left in our political views. We were probably in love with each other, but still too socially and religiously conditioned to see the truth of it. The contradictions were too difficult at that moment to sort out. It was for us an existential problem, not a political one. As we reminisced, I became acutely aware of the difficulty.

"God, Willie, why did we do it? I mean, look at us! What are we doing standing here in this uniform waiting for them to let us out? We both volunteered to go over there," I continued, emphasizing the word volunteered with a certain amount of amazement. "What were we thinking four years ago?"

Willie smiled at me, shrugged his shoulders and said in his usual, unperturbed, unflappable way, "Why do we do anything? It was the right thing at the right time, I guess."

"But we both hate the war," I said somewhat confrontationally. "We both hate Johnson and Nixon. So why did we ask to go?"

"Ah, I don't know anymore," Willie said almost absent-mindedly, and I couldn't remember anymore either. After a few moments of silence, he looked up and gave me a kind of answer.

"Because we're addicted to the adrenaline rush and running away from the boredom," Willie replied looking directly into my eyes. "Because maybe we have this ego problem that demanded we get involved in the historical significance of the whole thing. And because we were not aware enough of ourselves at the outset to take a moral stand."

I knew Willie was at least partly right. I knew the military experience was an attempt to resolve some of my personal problems, and in many ways I succeeded. Yet, I hadn't resolved them all. But Willie made me realize that we were lucky enough to have a war to run away to—not a circus, but a real war to break us out of the cocoon of childhood—a war to escape the dreadful social conformity and family expectations we so deeply feared, yet still couldn't quite escape—a war to find out what we were truly made of as men. It was an archetypal and primal male experience that connected us to the deepest levels of our being.

"I hate to admit it, Willie, but I miss it," I said wistfully.

"I know, I miss it sometimes, too," he said with a small shrug of his shoulders.

"Sometimes I really hate the World," I continued in a melancholic tone. The World was this normal place of human activity that paralleled our lives in Vietnam. While we were fighting, dying, being bored, crazy, frightened and self-indulgent, the people in the World were working nine-to-five, commuting, living standard American lives, only vaguely aware of our reality over there. It was superficial, neon, glitzy, shiny, cellophane-wrapped and television-soaped. And I hated it. I wanted to shake it and shake it until it woke up and saw what was really happening.

"The World, huh?" repeated Willie with a half smile. "You mean the whole world or just the world outside of the Army?" He knew what I meant, but he was testing me in a way.

I thought it over and decided that, if I hated the whole world, self-hatred was included. That could be. If I hated just the world outside of the Army, I might as well re-enlist right away. I really didn't hate myself that much and I couldn't possibly re-enlist. Smiling and looking a bit sheepish, I said, "OK, guess I was being a bit overly dramatic. Sorry."

"Aw, we'll get used to the World again. It just takes time." Willie was comforting me and his voice revealed the depth of his affection.

"I suppose," I said unconvinced. "I guess I'm wondering if that's what I want."

"Just think," said Willie trying to hard to be positive, "one minute we're in uniform, saluting, putting up with inspections and all the bullshit and real soon now we'll be free to think individually and not worry where our weapon is or whether the next person we see requires a salute. God, it's a whole new life!"

I smiled at the thought, but felt a tinge of discomfort and anxiety, too. I looked up at Willie and he looked back, raising his fist in the air and looking down. It always made me smile when he struck that Black Power pose. Somehow we identified strongly with the oppressed and we adopted that symbol as our own statement of resilience and resistance to being absorbed into the military mind. We stood in line quietly through the rest of the bureaucratic process. Periodically we'd make eye contact, smile briefly, nod and raise a silent fist over our heads. After our medical exams we signed our final papers and then we were civilians.

We had everything packed. It wasn't much. The total fit into the front trunk of Willie's new, blue Volkswagen bug. We had plans. A rock concert was scheduled at William and Mary College in Williamsburg and we had bought tickets. Traffic was the headliner with J.J. Cale and Redbone. Redbone stole the show in the smoky, frisbee-filled air. We climbed into Willie's new, blue Volkswagen after the concert and headed west.

It was just after midnight. We were high from the marijuana, rock music and the energy inside the concert hall. The world was starry bright and my mind was free and open. The vibration of the car pacified me as I curled up in the seat. Security and comfort spread through my limbs as anger and fear had done so often during the previous four years. I looked over at Willie's face staring through the windshield into the night. The shadows of his nose, chin and gentle eyes contrasted sharply with the brightness of the headlights from the on-coming traffic. The stark black and white image etched itself in my feelings and a strong wave of emotion began to well up inside of me.

I wanted to tell Willie how much I cared about our friendship and our experiences together...how much I loved him. But such words wouldn't form on my lips for fear they would be misunderstood, or maybe reciprocated. Either way, I wasn't ready to deal with it. I controlled myself quietly for a few moments until Willie broke the stillness.

Reaching into his shirt pocket Willie said, "Here. Want one of these?"

"What is it?" I asked leaning slightly forward to get a better look.

"It's a christmas tree," he answered with a chuckle. He smiled slyly, yet there was a spark of friendliness and nurturing in his expression.

I was a little puzzled. "I don't get it."

"It's amphetamine," announced Willie matter-of-factly. "The medic at Fort Meade gave me a congratulatory short supply as a going away present when I got my physical. It's green and white, so it's called a christmas tree."

It struck me as perfect. I didn't want to sleep anyway. We were hurling through the night, speeding further and further away from a painful past and breaking through to a wide-open future. I didn't want to miss a thing. We both wanted to explore this new sense of freedom, yet we were both also slightly unnerved by the sense of being cast adrift in the World. The sensation of being out of the Army was thick and tangible. We had grown accustomed to being completely enveloped by the military matrix—led here and there—told what to do. We were used to ourselves in a very ordered world. Now we had suddenly been released into a world where any order to life came from within and was not absolutely imposed from without. We wanted to escape from the constraints of the past few years in the military, but we both keenly felt the anxiety of this panoramic openness outside of the Army.

We sat quietly in our seats, each in our own separate space trying to adjust to these new circumstances. The effects of the speed began to take hold and the speeding drug began to match the momentum of the speeding car, dissolving the barriers between us, at least for a while. I realized that Willie had been feeling as emotional and confused as I had, but like me could not communicate it. With the barriers gone the psychological atmosphere changed. We talked. We laughed. We explored the universe within each other and wrapped ribbons of highway around steel-belted radials.

We finally stopped for food and coffee at a truck stop somewhere in West Virginia. We ended up laughing at ourselves and at our discomfort eating breakfast alongside leather-faced truckers with southern accents, cracking suggestive jokes at the waitresses—country-western women in crisp pastel with helmets of freshly sprayed hair piled high in swirls and engineered with bobbypins. Our speed-induced perceptions created a Marx Brothers' dialogue in southern accent out of the many peripheral conversations. We couldn't relate. With very wide grins and overly alert eyes, we walked back to the car and continued the journey westward. Willie wanted to visit his family in Mineral Wells, Texas. I had applied to college in Olympia, Washington and sooner or later needed to arrive there. For now, though, time didn't exist. There was only impulsive movement with no thought of limitations or responsibility.

"Hey," said Willie, "let's go to Markham, Texas and visit Jim Polk."

"Jim Polk? Ahh, sure, OK," I agreed. "Why not? You know where it is?"

"Somewhere down outside of Houston near the coast," he replied. "I think Jim should be there. He got out...let's see...just before Christmas, didn't he?"

"Yeah, he did." I stopped to think about Jim and chuckled. "He's incredible, y'know? I've had some really interesting conversations with him."

"Me, too." added Willie. "I always thought he was one of the more intelligent guys

I met in the Army."

"Yup," I said, "pretty smart guy. He got kinda crazy though towards the end. I think it finally got to him a little. He was doing too many drugs there for awhile."

"Well, yeah, he started feeling the pressure, I think," agreed Willie. "Crazy and intelligent went hand in hand for a lot of guys. I'd really like to see him again, though. But in his own space, y'know?"

"OK, let's go," I said. So we decided to head for the Southwest. Dawn broke through behind us and the rays of the sun seemed to energize Willie's speeding, blue, German machine. West Virginia sped by Kentucky and Tennessee. Mississippi disappeared into Louisiana and East Texas, and Houston appeared sprawling across the flatness of the Coastal Plains. Next stop: Markham.

Markham was this quiet, musty little town outside of Bay City. Clearly, there wasn't much prosperity there. Willie had the address and soon we pulled into a dirt driveway at the end of which was a small, green tarpapered house. It could've been a 1935 depression–era scene. Nothing had changed here in a long, long time. Jim emerged from behind the little house, noticed the car and walked toward us. His face clearly communicated the fact he had no idea who we were or why we were there. Once he recognized us, his expression changed, he smiled and picked up his pace across the overgrown yard.

Willie and I stayed seated in the car. We had anticipated spending some time with Jim, but we were stunned by his family's apparent poverty. Jim leaned with his fore arms against the driver's side.

"I can't believe it!" he exclaimed in his coastal Texan drawl. "You guys lost or what?"

Willie answered first. "Naw, headin" home and thought we'd stop by and see you—just say hello."

"Well, y'all sure surprised me," Jim said with a smile. "So, what's up? What're y'all gonna to do now that you're out?"

I shrugged my shoulders a bit and said, "Go back to school, I guess. Have to do something with my life. How about yourself?"

"Make a life here," Jim answered gesturing with his head to indicate the house and town. "It ain't much, I guess, but it's home, y'know? I'll find work in Bay City or something. You going back home, too, Willie?"

"Well, just to visit, I think." Willie answered. "I'm not sure where I'll end up. For sure not in Texas, but I don't know yet."

Jim nodded his head, turned and exhaled so we could hear it. The conversation came to an abrupt end. Jim looked back in the car window at us and said, "Why don't y'all come in. I'll gitcha a beer."

Willie looked over at me and I saw no willingness in his face to get out of the car. I didn't have the desire either to go in the house. Neither of us wanted to spend any more time there.

"Uh, thanks, but I think we gotta split. Still have to drive up to Mineral Wells. Haven't seen the family in awhile...you know," said Willie obviously creating excuses.

"Yeah," Jim said, "it's a stretch...well, OK, then, ah, look..." he continued struggling for words, slapped the door frame lightly and said, "It was good to see y'all...

take care, huh?"

"Yeah, sure," Willie responded, "you, too. Sorry we can't stay longer...it's been awhile, y'know?" I sat completely silent. I didn't know what to say. Jim just wasn't as I imagined he would be.

"Thanks for stoppin' by," said Jim stepping back away from the car. "I gotta go pick up my mom down at the post office, anyway. Good to see y'all. Y'all are some crazy sumbitches to drive all the way down here just to say hello!"

I just smiled and nodded my head in Jim's direction. Jim turned around and disappeared into the little house. Willie turned on the ignition and pulled out of the dirt driveway. Neither of us spoke for some time as we headed down the highway out of town. We were both trying to sort out the experience. I felt as if we were intruding. Jim was so simple and uncomplicated in his own element—even sedate. Perhaps it was merely the austerity, but we had known him and experienced him as vibrant—a bonvivant really with remarkable humor and intelligence. Yet here he was telling us that was all the past and now he wanted to return to a simple, uncomplicated, church-on-Sunday life in a small Texas town.

Willie turned to me and said, "Y'know, he has ten brothers and sisters and a mother and father who all live in that little place."

I felt a sadness come over me. I looked out at the local scenery and the geography was reminiscent of the Mekong Delta. As we passed by shanties and old, run down houses I felt the similarity of my early childhood in the rural Midwest, life in Vietnam and the local landscape. They were all fertile wastelands and it was life in the margins. I saw it all as an emblem of the moral poverty and injustice of the war and America with all of its contradictions. I realized I had always lived in the margins of society and so had Jim. I then began to understand why Jim wanted to stay there. It was for the same reason Willie and I had wanted to stay in Vietnam. It was existence on the edge of life. There was no real comfort and ease, but rather continual struggle to survive materially, emotionally and spiritually. Simply, I felt alive and independent. I felt my own person. I felt exhilarated and focused—not bored and conformed. There is no mainstream of society in the margins.

I looked over at Willie and saw in his face the same contemplation and perhaps sadness. A flood of memories filled me. I didn't want to lose them or my friendship with Willie. I wanted to reach out and hold him. I had learned to hate so strongly in the military and whatever feelings of love and affection I had were pushing up, breaking through, threatening to destroy the last four years of conditioning. I had wanted this breakthrough, but now I was panicking. Willie looked over at me and I could see that he, too, was struggling with his own thoughts and perceptions. We never spoke. Neither of us could let it out, even to talk about. We were so bonded together, yet our relationship was so frightening to us that we couldn't express our mutual respect and affection. Macho grew in the land. The Texas sky fell over us and we grew hard against the emerging desert.

I knew then that our separation was near and we couldn't say to each other that it mattered or that we cared. We were in love and afraid of the emotion. We refused to risk exposing ourselves. We had sped through the sound barrier from Vietnam to the States and the concussion shattered our link. We lost each other somewhere in the wastelands of West Texas in an inertial plunge into old adolescent ways of being.

"I think I'll go back to D.C.," said Willie suddenly, cutting through the silence. "I kinda like it there...find a place in Virginia, get a job..."

"Wow," I said without enthusiasm or energy. "I guess we need to make some decisions then about where we're going next."

"I need to see my parents," said Willie. "You can come with me or whatever you wanna do."

I thought it over a few seconds and realized I would be prolonging the inevitable by going on to Mineral Wells. I needed to make this separation a clean break—a simple, matter-of-fact, unemotional, everyday, see-ya-later. I took a deep breath, let it out and said, "Maybe I'll just catch the bus home. I need to get there soon anyway and get my life squared away before I start college in March."

Willie didn't say anything for a while. I could see him thinking. He finally said, "I'll drop you off at the bus station then in Fort Worth and just head home from there."

"Great," I responded. "Works for me." We then sat in the car in silence again. I became very depressed as we drove closer to Fort Worth. Once we were in the city, I started gathering my things from the back seat. We still weren't talking much. Willie had the radio on listening to music to avoid any real interaction.

We pulled into the bus station and crawled out of the little car. Willie pulled open the hood of the front trunk and I gathered my things from inside. "There," I said, "got it all."

Our good-bye was sufficiently cool: a stiff handshake, a protective guffaw, an expectedly unfulfilled promise to write, and a take-care. I felt miserable. I needed to tell Willie how I felt, how much I loved him, but I was scared and unwilling.

After buying my ticket, we walked silently together up to the parked bus and stood there not looking at each other. Willie was fidgeting slightly with his hands in his front pockets. The driver began taking passengers' tickets and helping them up the steps into the bus. We moved aside waiting until the last possible moment to say the final good-bye. I was so intensely involved in controlling my emotions that I couldn't speak. As the last person boarded, I felt almost desparate and looked over at the bus then back at Willie. Willie clenched his hands in his pockets and wouldn't look up. But it was time. Willie wasn't going to say anything, so I began walking toward the door of the bus. I decided that I had to say something. I simply didn't want to leave like this—so abruptly and coldly. Knowing that I might never see him again gave me the courage to tell him how I felt. I stopped, turned around and walked back toward him. I put my things on the ground at his feet and placed my right hand on his chest, looking directly into his eyes. I could feel the warmth of his body through the shirt as I pressed my fingers against his body. I was regretting deeply that I hadn't expressed to him how much his friendship meant to me.

"I'll miss you. You know that," I said quietly but firmly.

Willie's eyes began to tear and his lower lip quivered slightly. He placed his hand over mine and nodded his head, but said nothing. He couldn't say anything. The raw emotion was right at the surface and any words would have subverted his control. Realizing his emotional state, I looked at him with all the affection I felt and silently mouthed the words, "I love you." His expression changed from grief to surprise then he smiled only slightly and nodded his head. I dropped my hand, picked up my things and walked back to the bus. I looked briefly over my shoulder at Willie as I climbed up the steps. He was standing there just staring back at me. I nodded my head in his direction in a final goodbye and disappeared into the bus.

Finding a seat was easier than fighting back the grief I felt. I stuffed my things above me and below me, then sat down. I looked out the window as the bus lurched forward. I saw Willie through the dirty glass and aluminum frame of the Trailways bus. He was leaning in his typical Willie pose against his new, blue Volkswagen now covered in red Texas dirt. He raised a silent fist in the air and hung his head. The bus pulled away in slow motion and I closed my eyes to shut out the world.

Sometime later I awoke to the hum of the engine lulling passengers to an uncomfortable sleep. It was the middle of the night. I stared out the window but couldn't make much out of the terrain in the dark. I leaned back, closed my eyes and recalled the image of Willie driving at night through West Virginia. I shook off the impending emotion and fell back asleep. I knew that when I awoke it would be a new day and time for both Willie and me—a new beginning. The Army had been the backdrop for our friendship and without the war our choices had become polarized. Willie chose the East; I had chosen the West. Though intimately together for so long, our paths finally parted.

Two days later I stepped off the bus into a cool Pacific Northwest drizzle. The wet pavement reflected the silver sky and the reflection served as a mirror. I saw Vietnam moving inside me and I was molded by it. I saw Willie inside me, and I was humanized. I suddenly realized that Willie would always be a brother and friend, whether we saw each other again or not. I realized my part in the war was over and it would slowly lose its hold on me. It was February 1972, the sun was in Aquarius and I had finally come home.

# Afterword

While in Vietnam, I kept looking for men who had the same reasons I did for not dodging or evading the draft and I found many. For some it was patriotism, but not for most. Now, with the U.S. involved in the Middle East, I hear echoes of the old love it or leave it sentiment—you're either with us or against us—and the politically correct refrain to support the troops regardless of your view of the war. I also hear among today's war veterans that they volunteered for family, God, country, duty, etc. I was 18 years old when I went to Vietnam. To be perfectly honest, I knew very little about God, country and duty in the way I hear it today and the way people mean it.

I had absolutely no sense of being "American." That national identity took many years of education and studying American history to form. I was just a kid from a relatively small town somewhere in the United States. In my mind I could've been born in Russia or Germany or Iceland...it was strictly an accident of history that I was born in Casper, Wyo., and I had no emotional or psychological attachment to fighting or warring out of duty to America, God and family. That never entered my head. I grew up with a strong work-ethic and sense of service to family and neighborhood, but I did not consciously say it was 'my duty' to work hard or be of help to others. I did not objectify those things that way. It was simply my will. It came from within me, not imposed as a social value from outside of me. I went to Vietnam simply because it was my will to do so and that was that.

I don't remember ever talking to anyone who went to Vietnam out of a sense of "duty." If they were drafted, I often heard this: "it's what you're supposed to do when you get called...you go." Well, that's not Duty, that's resignation and rather mindless acceptance of fate...which is ok...it's neither here nor there...but let's not call it Duty or some quasi-spiritual nationalism or even patriotism. I am sure there were soldiers who had a sincere sense of patriotism, but I didn't, because I didn't know emotionally what that was. I knew intellectually what patriotism was, but I had no real grasp of it personally and I did not feel it. If a soldier was Regular Army (volunteer enlistment), he did it because he liked the idea of the military or he was in search of something outside of himself—or maybe even inside of himself. Sometimes it was family tradition and sometimes it was family pressure to do something 'honorable.' But seldom was the reason for going a matter of personal Honor, Duty and Love of Country. For some it was political and ideological—capitalism vs communism—stop the dominoes from falling, that sort of thing. For the gay men, it was more complex. Some wanted to prove themselves as men, others were more like me—they just wanted to prove themselves, period. Being a male or gay or straight was never the issue. Whatever it was, it was deeply rooted in our psychology and the war experience brought it to the surface and forced us to deal with it.

I did not get drafted; I joined. And I volunteered to stay in Vietnam after my first tour was finished. I'll be the first to tell anyone who asks, however, that it had nothing whatsoever to do with patriotism, nationalism, God, family, country or some mystical notion of Duty. At the time it was completely irrational. I had no rational reason for joining (I didn't have to and I probably wouldn't have been drafted), and I had no rational reason for extending in Vietnam. It was simply a place to be other than in school or in the family. It was escape; it was living on the edge where life and death mattered; it was to remove myself from the mainstream of cultural life of America in 1968 and follow my young, boyish heart seeking that archetypal Circus. I was playing the Fool, knapsack on my back stepping off the cliff chasing a butterfly with the hounds of social convention, conformity and my personal history nipping at my heels.

The fact that there was a War made the adventure that much more significant to me. It was historically meaningful and I could work out my existential problems at the same time. If I died, which was a possibility, then I died. I wasn't terribly interested in gathering the forces around me to protect myself from potential death. I wouldn't have joined, if that had been the case. Death didn't frighten me that way. I was 18 and invulnerable. That doesn't mean I was brave! That just means I was unconscious of it and ignorant—I ignored the reality of Death, but kept my feelers out waiting for it, just in case it came by.

So, draft-dodgers and evaders...well, they had their own problems to work out. They did what they did for their own personal reasons, the same as those of us who went. It isn't for any one of us to judge them. They did us no harm. And as for the prejudice we received as Vietnam Vets, well, that was the nature of the World then.

The World, remember, was this general term for all life outside of our experience in Vietnam—and it was extremely difficult for all of us to enter the World as abruptly as we were forced to after returning to the States. We saw people conducting their normal, everyday life, work, relationships, families, etc. and we stood there in our jungle fatigues blankly staring at them. They looked back with the same lack of understanding. I remember wanting to get their attention, but they ignored me, or worse, called me names (although no one ever spit at me). I wanted to grab them and shake them and scream, "Hey, wake up!! You're asleep...there's a War going on and look at you! You're acting as if it's not! I know, I was there and there's a War going on. I know that guys are dying!" But only the so-called 'crazy, radical, anti-war hippies' took me seriously, because that was the nature of the World at that time. The 'Silent Majority' remained relatively silent because you didn't criticize the country while it was at war. That was the nature of the World, too. But I was of the nature of Vietnam and it had molded me into a different person.

Then I realized that I, the "Vietnam I," was invisible to all my friends and family. They could never know me there. If I was ever to be part of the World again, I had to adjust to that reality. I hated the World for that and it took me many years to able to forgive. But it was Reality with a giant R, and I saw other vets around me falling apart because they couldn't adapt. Dodgers and evaders were a part of the World, so it was easy to hate them, too. I work with them and live next door to them now. They are men with families, careers, lives, loves, failures and successes, just like me. We talk some now about Vietnam and our respective experiences—they had their own terrors. I don't feel sorry for them at all, but then I don't feel sorry for me either.

G.D. Lorentzen
Portland, Oregon

# About The Author

    G.D. Lorentzen was born in Wyoming and grew up there and in North Dakota until his family moved to the Puget Sound area of Washington State when he was 11. He was raised in a multicultural environment of Native Americans (Mandan, Hidatsa, Arikara), Germans from Russia and Scandinavians. Once he moved west away from that culture, he took his cowboy boots off and never put them back on. He knew he was gay at the age of ten, discussed it with his father briefly at the age of fourteen, joined the military at seventeen to discover and claim his masculinity. After that, he studied at the The Evergreen State College in Olympia, WA, the University of Washington in Seattle and Portland State Univesity in Portland, OR. He has a B.A. in Liberal Arts with a concentration in Buddhist Studies, Philosophy and Psychology, another major in History and Education and another in German with a Master's Degree in Germanics. He now lives happily with his partner of thirteen years in Portland, OR.

www.ingramcontent.com/pod-product-compliance
Lightning Source LLC
Chambersburg PA
CBHW050829180626
46814CB00004B/1524